He stood then, picking her up so that her legs wrapped around his waist. His lips crashed down over hers, his tongue plundering hers with deep thrusts and smooth strokes. His hands cupped her bottom, gripping each mound with the promise of more to come. Tia instinctively wrapped her arms around his neck, pressing her aching center into him, wanting more, needing it all.

She felt him move, turn in the opposite direction, but his hands were now pushing her dress up farther until he touched the bare flesh of her bottom, skimming the thin wisp of her thong. Her entire body shivered at the brief contact. She sighed and nipped his bottom lip.

"Which way?" he rasped.

Tia couldn't speak, but pointed toward the bedroom.

Books by A.C. Arthur

Kimani Romance

Love Me Like No Other
A Cinderella Affair
Guarding His Body
Second Chance, Baby
Defying Desire

A.C. ARTHUR

Artist C. Arthur was born and raised in Baltimore, Maryland, where she currently resides with her husband and three children. An active imagination and a love for reading encouraged her to begin writing in high school, and she hasn't stopped since. Determined to bring a new edge to romance, she continues to develop intriguing plots, racy characters and fresh dialogue—thus keeping readers on their toes! Visit her Web site at www.acarthur.net.

Defying DESIRE

A.C. Arthur

To the readers who couldn't wait to see Trent fall.

 KIMANI PRESS™

Recycling programs
for this product may
not exist in your area.

ISBN-13: 978-0-373-86109-5
ISBN-10:   0-373-86109-5

DEFYING DESIRE

www.kimanipress.com

Printed in U.S.A.

Dear Reader,

It's finally his turn!

The infamous, arrogant, sexy, domineering Trent Donovan is now in murky waters as his desire for Tia St. Claire has him doing the exact thing he'd ragged his brothers about: falling in love.

Trent is a good man; I think that was obvious in the way he showed his love and devotion for his brothers in *Love Me Like No Other* and *A Cinderella Affair*. He just had to find that special woman, one who could give him what he needed—in all areas. Tia is that woman. She can do a one-night stand, she can do nonchalant, she can take him or leave him. But she can also touch a part of him that no other woman has.

Defying Desire was an emotional story, but one with such a heartfelt ending that it had to be told. So enjoy Trent and then be on the lookout for the rest of the Donovan clan to find their love as well!

AC

Chapter 1

"You give new meaning to the word untamable," Lincoln Donovan said, chuckling as he opened the door to his truck and stepped inside.

"What?" Trenton Donovan opened the back door to his older brother's Suburban and tossed his bags on the floor. "You can't trust women. Adam's crazy ex Kim proved that point."

Trent climbed inside on the passenger side and pulled his seat belt across him as his older brother started the engine.

"All you had to do was have her checked out like you do everybody else. You didn't have to sleep with her and then walk out on her. And you said she had a child?" Lincoln asked.

Trent defended himself. "First of all, I didn't sleep with her and walk out. Lynn knew that I wasn't looking for anything long term. I told her as much when I realized we were feeling each other. And as for the kid, Jeremy was pretty cool. But where there's a child there's bound to be a daddy and that leads to trouble."

"Like I said, you could have just checked her out. You were working with her brother on a case so you probably shouldn't have messed with her in the first place. Sam Desdune is never going to ask for your help again," Linc chided.

Trent had thought the same thing himself after the one night he spent with Lynn, but by that point it was too late. To her credit, Lynn hadn't taken the night they'd celebrated the capture of her younger sister's stalker any more seriously than Trent had. Her own issues with her runaway ex-husband and her young son were her priorities, not trying to build something with Trent.

It had been an impulsive act, one that he regretted only in the sense that he'd used Lynn Desdune as a replacement for the one woman who continued to elude him.

They were driving down the highway on their way to the Donovan family estate. Henry and Beverly Donovan were fanatical about their family. And since Trent was the middle child, the renegade of the three sons formally dubbed the Triple Threat Donovans, they paid special attention to him.

After a two-month assignment in Connecticut, he'd recently returned home to Vegas and was welcomed by sonogram pictures of the twins growing in Jade's stomach. Jade and Linc had been married for almost six months and already she was pregnant. Linc was so excited he practically had father-to-be tattooed on his forehead.

Once at the estate Trent was sure that his younger brother Adam and his fiancée, Camille, would be there. Noelle, Jade's younger sister would come along sharing her latest escapade. Noelle was a burst of energy in the low-key Donovan household. However, Trent had to admit that her reckless nature was beginning to subside. He suspected Linc and the trust he showed by hiring her at the Gramercy Casino was the reason for that.

At any rate, the hot shower, spicy wings and stack of *Sports Illustrated* magazines waiting for him back at his townhouse would have to wait. Family was very important to him and he wanted to spend quality time with everyone especially since he'd just witnessed two close-knit families almost torn apart by revenge.

That reminded him that he needed to really give some thought to Sam Desdune's offer. Partnering with Sam and opening a P.I. agency on the West Coast was something he needed to seriously consider.

Trent and Sam had met years ago on an assignment for the military and remained close afterward. A former police officer in the sleepy town of Greenwich, Connecticut, Sam now owned his own P.I. firm. Trent had flown to the East Coast to assist Sam and one of his high-profile clients with a particularly sensitive investigation.

For twelve years Trent had been a Navy SEAL putting his life on the line to protect and serve his country. He loved his job and though he had officially left the Navy, he still accepted special assignments. That worried his mother, which he didn't like, but it was his life. If he didn't help fight everyone else's battles, what good would he be?

"Heads up," Linc said pulling into the driveway of the estate an hour later. "Camille's got a bone to pick with you."

"Camille? What did I do to her?"

Linc only shook his head laughing as he parked and stepped out of the truck. "Man, you just don't know. Women don't forget a thing."

Trent stopped listening to Linc's warning as they walked into the house. He was happy to be back in Vegas but there were some things he could do without.

Tia St. Claire's head pounded with what she knew would be a hellacious headache. She realized it was because the two-year "anniversary" of her accident was fast approaching. She couldn't help but count down these last dreaded days.

Last year at this time she'd been working, doing a runway show in Paris one night, then flying to Milan for one there and then coming back to L.A. for a photo shoot. In between she'd done promo shots to update her portfolio and met with her agent. She'd worked from January first straight through and past March second, the day of the accident. That had been the only way to cope with the pain—and using the jet lag as an excuse to sleep every hour that she wasn't modeling.

This year she was working again, but she wasn't traveling back and forth. And whenever she wasn't in front of the camera she was feeling the pain.

When she was finally alone in her apartment she slumped down into the nearest chair. With the backs of her hands she wiped her face clean only to have warm tears slip from her eyes again.

It wasn't her fault, she knew that. Jake had been driving and she'd been in the passenger seat. As if it were yesterday she heard the squeal of the tires, felt the uncontrollable spin of the car, the lurch of her heart in the precise moment the car slid into the tree. In an instant the two people that she loved most were gone—her fiancé, Jake, and their unborn daughter, Jessica.

Her life was spared although she had no idea why. Work was her only solace.

At least it had been.

She'd been modeling for so long that it was almost like breathing. So even though the photo shoots were normally filled with photographers, hairstylists, designers and the other people who just always seemed to be around either backstage or in the studio, Tia would usually sink into herself.

While her body moved, her mind functioned on autopilot and her thoughts and feelings were her own. That may seem weird to a novice but, for her, even walking down the runway provided solace to her tortured soul. The crowds were blurred out so that all she saw was the darkness, the same darkness that had engulfed the ones she'd loved. When she was on the runway, she was with Jake and Jessica.

Camille Davis was the phenomenal woman behind CK Davis Designs. Tia had been ecstatic when her agent had booked her for their fall fashion show. From there Camille had specifically requested her for other assignments until the bulk of Tia's time was now spent working for Camille and modeling her fabulous designs.

That, of course, was not the bad part. The irony came when Camille had introduced Tia to Adam and the rest of the Donovan family. They were a lively bunch with the seniors, Henry and Beverly, still madly in love after years of marriage. Jade and Linc were almost sickening to watch together, their happiness pouring from them in heavy waves. Then there was Camille herself and the infamous Adam Donovan. Their love was pure, of the fairy-tale type, the kind that little girls dreamed of.

Soon after they'd met, Camille had shared the story of how Adam had swept her off her feet like her very own Prince Charming, helping her to defeat her wicked stepmother and all. The love between the two of them was more than crystal clear, the fantasy, for them, more than real.

The dream Tia had once had.

The entire clan and their happiness exacerbated the fact that Tia was alone. She'd chosen to be alone, that was true, but she'd never felt its impact like she did these days. Once upon a time she'd wanted a husband and a family and that dream had quickly come crashing down, so it was her firm belief that those things were not meant for her. But every once in a while...

"Stop it," she berated herself and moved to the minirefrigerator. Yanking it open she retrieved a bottled water and unscrewed the top. She took three big gulps, then added a deep breath and felt herself calming considerably.

Tia really didn't begrudge the Donovans their happiness and she genuinely liked them all, well, she liked the majority of them.

The Donovans were a very reputable family in Las Vegas. Henry and Beverly Donovan both came from old money, circling back to oil rigs in Texas and global financiers. Now the retirees spent the majority of their time either traveling or promoting various charities and organizations that focused on topical issues such as health care for all, pediatric HIV/AIDS victims and domestic violence.

The family was well-known throughout the U.S., which made them and their offspring fair game to the media circus.

He was another matter all together.

Trenton Donovan, the middle child and last of the Triple Threat Donovan Brothers, at least that's what the papers called him. To Tia, he was just an arrogant pain in the ass.

He'd gotten her number from Camille and called Tia for two weeks straight after they'd had to model together in a charity fashion show last fall. Tia would readily admit that the man was fine. Hell, he was beyond fine. Tall, way over six feet, built like two average men combined to make one superhero-like body and a face that would make a woman wet just looking at him.

His skin was a soft mocha tone, his eyes dark and ominous. Not normally a woman fascinated by the facial features of a man, Tia had, however, committed Trent's features to memory. He was clean shaven, unlike his brothers. That should have given him a boyish look; instead, it enhanced his dangerous aura. A sharp chin and firm mouth made him always appear serious. His no-nonsense way of talking said he meant business all the time.

And Tia couldn't stand him.

She'd finally called him back after growing tired of his phone messages.

"I'm calling to inform you that stalking is punishable by jail time," she'd said the moment he answered the phone.

"Merry Christmas to you, too," he'd said, his voice sending a shiver down her spine.

Tia had tried like hell to keep her resolve. "If I wanted you to call me I would have given you my number. On second thought, if you wanted to call me you probably should have asked for my number instead of getting it from someone else."

"Wait a minute, are you upset about something?"

"Upset? That's an understatement. Normally a man asks my name and then asks for my number. I don't recall you doing, either."

"My soon-to-be sister-in-law is Camille Davis. She told me your name. And you were so busy with your little fan club at the party after the fashion show, I didn't get a chance to ask you anything."

She sighed deeply. "Be that as it may, I don't appreciate your uninvited phone calls. I want them to stop."

He'd grown silent and for a moment she thought he may have hung up on her.

But then he spoke again. "Why don't you take a minute to calm down and we'll start this conversation all over again."

"Why don't you get over yourself? Every woman is not ready to fall at your feet, nor are they excited by your initiative to get to know them better. And for the record, I'm one of them."

"Hold on a second. All I did was call to ask you out to dinner."

"And I just happened to be that woman? This week? I know how you work and I'm not buying it, so you can just find yourself another flavor of the month. As a matter of fact, did I ask you to call? Did I give you permission to call?"

"No, but—"

She cut him off. "Then I'd advise you not to call me anymore. It's as simple as that!"

Now, three months later, replaying the conversation in her head, she wondered if she had been a bit harsh. That wasn't normally her nature, but she didn't care. Trent Donovan was definitely used to getting what he wanted from women. And from the persistence in his voice on her answering machine she knew exactly what he wanted from her. Too bad he wasn't going to get it.

That last statement was easier for her to say than actually believe. Especially since she hadn't stopped thinking about him since the night of the fashion show. He was attractive, but that was an understatement—he was a Donovan after all. And while she normally wasn't that focused on what was going on around her as she worked, the moment he'd touched her she'd been more than aware of his presence. It had begun as a slow burn then moved through her until it was a full-blown tornado storming through her, demanding her attention.

Luckily the after party was crowded, affording her the perfect opportunity to put distance between herself and the renowned Mr. Donovan. She had no other choice. Tia had learned her lesson: it was much better to be safe than sorry.

Chapter 2

"Whatever you said to her it couldn't have been nice because the next day when I mentioned your name she almost bit my head off." Camille Davis sat in a high-backed chair near the book shelf in the den of the Donovan estate.

Trent had been back at his childhood home for less than an hour and was already being chewed out by his brother's fiancée. He liked Camille. She'd had a rough childhood and a witch of a stepmother. Her Hollywood producer father had died and through her grief she'd managed to grow up, attend college and build her own fashion empire.

Now she was engaged to Adam, his younger brother. Trent never thought Adam would get married. Then again, none of his brothers were supposed to get married. But ever since Linc had copped out and proposed to Jade, the Triple Threat Brothers had been in trouble.

It was up to Trent to stick to his guns. He didn't trust women, that was number one. And there were more than a few that had proven his nontrust theory—Adam's ex Kim, who had teamed up with Camille's stepmother to break them up, undoubtedly came to mind.

No, Trent liked the company of women on a temporary basis. Anything beyond that was out of the question. Besides, he lived a dangerous life. One that worried his family constantly. Trent wasn't about to put a wife and kids through that same ordeal.

"Hey, she's the one who called me ranting and raving about rudeness and uninvited calls. I barely got a word in before she hung up on me," he said defending his three-month old conversation with Tia St. Claire. It didn't help that each time he saw a magazine cover or a CK Davis ad, it was Tia's face that was smiling back at him.

"You were probably your normal arrogant self," Camille quipped, then shook her head. "I should have never given you her number."

"Whose?" Adam said coming to stand next to Camille.

Trent frowned as he watched his brother's hand find Camille's shoulder. Camille looked up at him and smiled. Their gazes locked as if they hadn't seen each other in weeks. This was just the type of sappy crap he didn't have time for.

"Tia St. Claire," Camille answered.

"You're still after her? It's been months since the show. If you haven't hooked up with her yet it might be time to let it go."

Linc came up from behind Trent clapping him on his shoulder before he could respond to Adam's remark. "What's the matter? You losing your touch, bro?"

Trent gave them both a scowl. "Hell no, I'm not losing

my touch. I called her a couple of times and when she called back she was a royal—"

"Don't you dare call her out of her name," Camille admonished.

She was small and a little on the shy side, but man, she could reprimand him with a tongue-lashing as swift as his mother. That was only one of the things Trent liked about her.

"She was not a nice lady," he corrected and looked to Camille with a smirk for her approval. She smiled in return.

"I haven't talked to her since then," he finished.

"That's probably because it sounds like she doesn't want to have anything to do with you," Linc's wife, Jade, smirked, happily munching on a bowl of grapes as she sat, feet propped up, on the chaise lounge.

Trent didn't like the direction this conversation was taking. His brothers accusing him of losing his touch and his sisters-in-law claiming a victory for womankind. "Look, nothing happened between us which was probably for the best. It's over."

"Well, she's still pissed," Camille said.

Trent shrugged. "That's her problem." He went to the bar to fix himself a drink.

"It doesn't matter. Trent's been all the way to the East Coast breaking hearts. He can't possibly have time to worry about the ones he left here." Linc chuckled as he sat next to his wife, leaning over to kiss her cheek.

"Oh my, tell me it's not so." Camille sighed. "You were supposed to be working in Connecticut, not screwing."

At her last words everyone in the room looked in her direction. Camille Davis did not talk like that. Adam must really be rubbing off on her.

"I wasn't 'screwing' as you put it. I was helping a friend with a case."

"Right. Sam's case?" Adam said. "I remember him from last year when he came to visit you. Mom told me that's where you went."

"Sam's sister was the one Trent got with," Linc offered happily.

Trent tossed him a heated glare. "Her name was Lynn."

"And did you sleep with this Lynn?" Jade asked.

Jade was a pretty woman and now that she was pregnant her beauty had magnified. Her hazel eyes beamed while auburn curls hung just past her shoulders. And she made his brother Linc happier than Trent had ever seen him.

"I don't have to tell you people all the details of my sex life. Just know that Lynn and I are both adults. Whatever went down with us was absolutely consensual."

"He screwed her," Adam said looking across the room at Trent with a huge grin.

"You guys really need to get a life," Trent said before downing his drink.

Camille had asked Tia to meet her in her office after they'd gone over the proofs of last week's pictures, and as badly as Tia had wanted to beg off, she now found herself front and center with Camille, standing near one of the curtainless windows.

Tia now searched for a good enough reason to turn her boss and new friend down. For as much as she liked Camille, liked working for her, as well as spending time with her, she did not want to go to a party at the house she and Adam Donovan shared.

No Donovan party, *anywhere*.

It was too close to all the things that rubbed her the wrong way. All the little memories of the life she almost had were just too much to bear. It wasn't Camille's fault she'd found a great man to love her. And it wasn't Jade's fault that she and Linc had found each other after all those years, had gotten married and were now expecting twins. Just like it wasn't her fault that Jake and Jessica had died.

Blame was a useless emotion. She'd learned that well after the accident. But grief, it stayed with you no matter what. Weighing like a rope of bricks wrapped securely around her neck. And no matter how many assignments she took to keep her mind off it, grief held her down at every opportunity.

"It's a big night for both of us, Tia. I need you to be there," Camille continued pleading her case.

Dana, Camille's best friend and business partner, was sitting at her desk, trying not to gloat over all the orders that had come in, but offered her two cents readily. "In the last three months you've become the face of CK Davis Designs. We're opening our very first store so it's only logical—and expected—that you would be there."

"Ganging up on me is not going to work," Tia hissed.

"You're right," Dana agreed. "Oh, did I mention that if you don't show you're fired?"

Camille grinned. "Yep. It's part of your contract."

"That's a lie," Tia quipped. "Look, there's a really a good reason why I don't want to go."

"You don't want to run into Trent Donovan. We already know you despise him. Besides, he probably won't even be there," Dana said.

"I do not despise him," Tia argued.

"At any rate, Dana's right, he probably won't be there."

Probably? "I thought you said a while back he was out of town?" Tia said before she could stop herself.

Dana smiled sweetly. "Keeping tabs on him, are we?"

"No. Of course not. My reasons for not coming to the

party don't have anything to do with Trent. It's something personal."

Camille touched Tia's hand. "Okay. I can respect that. But I'd really like you to be there. Just for a little while. Then you can go back to your lonely little apartment."

Tia hated when Camille referred to her home as a lonely little apartment. The fact that her assessment wasn't far off the mark could be the reason. With the money she was making she could afford to buy herself a house. But that said permanency, it said planting roots and family…and all the things she'd had and lost.

"All right, I'll come. But I'm not staying long."

"Great!" Camille got up from her seat hugging Tia enthusiastically.

Tia could do nothing but hug her back. Besides she didn't get hugs often and this one felt genuine, like there was someone finally there for her.

Shaking her head she dismissed that notion. She didn't have close friends because she didn't want the connection. The more people in her life that she loved, the harder it would be if she lost them. Her only family, her parents, were still alive and living in Phoenix. That was enough anticipated heartache for her to carry.

Still, she couldn't help but like Camille. Just like she couldn't help but see the way Camille always looked at her, as if they shared a deep, dark secret. But that was impossible. Camille had no way of knowing what had happened to her two years ago and Tia had no intention of ever telling her.

"Do me a favor," Camille said finally releasing her. "Wear the black sheath. I have a great choker to go with it. Don't worry about driving, I'll send a car for you so you can get to the house a little early. I want the necklace on you before the paparazzi arrives."

"Sure. Why not? I have nothing else to do," she said dismally then mustered up a smile when Camille gave her another sympathetic look.

Before Camille could say another word Tia bent down, scooped up her purse and headed for the door. "I'll see you tomorrow night."

Tia was out the door and on the elevator before she released the breath she held. Slipups like that would only make things worse. She wasn't depressed and she didn't need anybody's pity, despite what her mother thought. She was coping with her loss in her own way and it was working just fine.

"What is up with her?" Dana asked when Tia had closed the door behind her.

Camille continued to stare at the spot where Tia St. Claire had stood. She was a beautiful woman, tall, thin and oozing sex appeal. All attributes most women would die for, yet she wore them more like a burden then a badge.

Tia was a fantastic model, whether runway or in print. She enhanced CK Davis Design's couture line and added a simple flair to the casual, ready-to-wear line. She was easy to work with and a pleasure to be around. But, Camille thought with a pang in her chest, Tia was the saddest person she'd ever met.

"I don't know. But I've got a feeling it's only a matter of time before it comes out."

"You think she's hiding something?"

"I know she is."

Dana sat back in her chair and finally turned to Camille.

"Do you think it's something that will hurt the company? Because if so we should probably cut our losses now."

Leave it to Dana to be concerned with business first.

That's why they were partners, Dana dealt with all the unsavory stuff while Camille worked her personable magic as frequently as possible.

Where Tia was concerned, Camille was almost positive Dana's way of thinking wasn't necessary.

She shook her head negatively. "Whatever it is, it's hurting her more than it could possibly hurt anyone else. Just leave her to me. I'll take care of it."

"Suit yourself," Dana quipped. "But if it starts to go bad, I'm axing her. We've worked too hard to have a model's baggage bring us down."

"Tia will be fine. I've got a sinking feeling we're going to end up helping her much more than she's helping us."

Chapter 3

Trent couldn't believe it. After three months away and being with other women, Tia still had his blood pumping when she entered a room.

Sipping on a rum and coke, he watched Tia St. Claire walk into Adam and Camille's home like a lion eyeing his prey. Earlier today he'd had a fleeting thought that she might show up tonight. CK Davis Designs new store would definitely open more doors for her as their top model, so of course she would come.

For him, it was once again about family. He was as proud of Camille and her company as if she were his blood sister. And he knew what it meant for Adam to see his fiancée finally happy with herself and her accomplishments. So he was here to show his support.

But with every step Tia took, every time her long honey-toned leg slipped through that sinful split up the left side of her dress, his hunger for Tia St. Claire grew.

Her hair was braided this time. It had been loose and curled when he'd last seen her. But the array of tiny braids in a mixture of gold and brownish tint pulled up into a neat bun showcasing her long, sensuous neckline was just as alluring. Somebody spoke to her and she smiled. Trent's chest constricted.

Her eyes, the color of warm honey, cased the room as she moved slowly, tentatively through the crowd. Her dress, the wicked creation he knew had to be one of Camille's designs, was black and held up by two tiny straps at the cap of her shoulders. Her breasts were high and looked full enough to fit his hands just perfectly. The seductive way she was walking had to be a crime in at least ten states. He was getting hard just looking at her move.

Usually his attraction to a woman was a slow simmer, edging him along until he was finally in her bed. But each time he saw Tia, his need for her burned instantly, intensely.

Camille entered and moved quickly to Tia. Tia turned giving Trent a full view of the back of the deadly dress, or should he say the lack of dress. In about two seconds he took in the fact that those small straps at her shoulders draped down the sides of her back, leaving what looked like miles and miles of titillating bronze skin open for all to see. The black material met again in a gentle gathering at the base of her back.

Trent almost groaned out loud. Instead, he emptied his glass and was turning to head straight to the bar for a refill when he bumped into Adam.

"She looks great, doesn't she?" his younger brother said with a grin on his face as broad as a Cheshire cat's.

Trent cleared his throat and took a step back. "Yeah. Camille's as pretty as a picture. I'm proud of your good taste, little bro."

He circled around Adam making a beeline for the bar. Unfortunately, Adam had decided to follow him.

"I wasn't talking about Camille. But thanks anyway."

Trent shook his head. He was not about to get into this with Adam. He knew exactly where his brother's joking tone was leading. "The boutique's going to be a big hit," Trent said when they'd made it to the bar and he'd given his glass to the bartender with a nod for a refill.

"Yeah," Adam agreed.

"Is that all you're going to say tonight?" Trent asked with agitation.

Adam simply chuckled. "She's doing one amazing number on you."

"What? Who?" Even to Trent's own ears the feigned innocence was unbelievable.

"You know who. Why don't you just go and talk to her?"

Trent shook his head. "No. The last thing I want for Camille tonight is a shouting match between me and her top model."

"Then don't shout at her."

"Me?" he asked touching a hand to his chest as if offended. "She's the one that called, cursing me out."

"You were being pushy and presumptuous with her. You should probably apologize."

"'Pushy and presumptuous'? If that doesn't sound like some female crap. You've been talking to Camille way too much."

"Nah," Adam said taking a glass of champagne from the tray one of the hostesses was carrying around. "I just see what she was saying. You come on to women really strong, Trent. And Tia strikes me as being different from the females you usually try to push up on."

"How? She's attractive and available just like the others," Trent quipped.

Adam chuckled. "For one, she's not falling all over you. I know you, you're used to women dying to meet the great Trent Donovan."

"Man, you know I don't even fall for that act. It's not me they're trying to meet, more like my wallet they're trying to get hold of."

"But you still like the attention. And she's the first woman to put you in your place right off the bat. She's got guts and intelligence. Not normally two traits you look for in a woman."

Trent thought about rebutting that statement but could only ask, "Whose side are you on? I mean, I know you're in love and about to get married and all that, but you were once where I am. When you saw something you wanted, you just went after it. We're Donovans, that's what we do."

"Until the right woman comes along and makes you *rethink* what we do," Adam said simply, his gaze crossing the room to where Camille stood.

Trent took a quick gulp of the drink the bartender had just given him. "See, I'm not even looking for that commitment you and Linc seem so happy to jump into these days. I was just trying for a good time with Tia. But if Miss Supermodel isn't interested then so be it."

Adam shook his head and began to walk away. Then he stopped and turned back to Trent. "I'll bet you five dollars you can't stay away from her all night."

"I don't gamble," Trent said seriously.

"No. You don't give up." With that said Adam went to stand by Camille, kissing her on her cheek as he glanced back across the room issuing a silent challenge to Trent.

* * *

She'd seen him and her stomach had done an immediate somersault. Yet Tia had refused to cower. His eyes were on her, hot and persistent, searing into every exposed inch of her skin. But she held her smile in place, moving and talking with people as if he weren't even in the room.

Which proved to be totally unsuccessful.

Even now Camille was saying something, the ever handsome and charming Adam right by her side, and Tia had no idea what she was talking about. Her back was to Trent but he was still watching her. She could feel it in every pore of her body.

"That choker is exquisite with the dress, Tia. Now, since this is just the preamble to the big launch party I've only invited a few top reporters. There's maybe one or two photographers moving about. So if you could make the rounds I'm sure they'll see you."

Tia's hand shook as she reached for a glass of champagne. She prayed nobody saw it; however, the hostess, who was about two inches shorter than her, smiled knowingly. Suddenly very thirsty, Tia lifted the glass to her lips and emptied the contents, the champagne leaving a tingling trail of chilliness down her throat.

"Hey? You okay?" Camille asked touching a hand to her wrist as she brought the empty glass away from her lips.

"I'm fine," Tia said trying to clear her head. If she thought of tonight as work she could probably make it through. If she didn't let herself remember that in just a couple of hours the anniversary date and time of the worst moment of her life would be upon her, she would be all right.

But then she heard his voice.

"She certainly is fine."

Oh God. Who am I fooling? I'm not going to make it. Trent Donovan was not going to let her get through this night unscathed. She could hear it in his voice even before she turned to look at him.

"Trent, I'm sure you remember my top model, Tia St. Claire," Camille said in a tight voice that dared Trent to misbehave.

That left Tia to wonder if she had recently been the topic of conversation in the Donovan household.

"How could I ever forget her?" He reached for her then, surprising her when he only took the empty glass out of her hand.

To her dismay, another hostess miraculously appeared and he disposed of the glass. Turning back to her, Trent took her hand in his. It was a move that looked practiced and smooth as hell all at the same time. Damn, she hated this man.

"How have you been, Tia?"

Okay, first he needed to stop touching her. Even the gentle feel of her hand in his and the thumb he caressed over her long, tapering fingers, was too much for her already quivering insides to take.

"I've been just fine. And you?" Her voice was steady even if the rest of her wasn't. And she didn't yank her hand out of his no matter how much she wanted to.

As Camille had said, reporters and photographers were here. She couldn't make a scene. The way Trent was looking at her said he'd figured that out before approaching her.

"I've been better."

I'll just bet you have. "That's nice. Now if you will all excuse me, I think I'll make my rounds now."

"That's a good idea," Camille chimed in. "Isn't it, Adam?"

Adam cleared his throat after Camille elbowed him in the ribs. "Ah, yeah. Good idea. How about I escort you out onto the terrace? I think Nigella from the *Chronicle* is out there soaking up the breeze."

Tia gladly accepted Adam's invitation but didn't miss the heated glare that passed between the two brothers as she did so. Refusing to even look back at Trent she made a hasty, but classy, retreat.

"Whatever you're thinking I want you to get it out of your mind right this minute," Camille said to Trent when they were alone.

"Why does everybody insist on treating me like I'm the bad guy?"

"Um, because you're military trained to take no prisoners."

Trent had to smile at that one. "She's a grown woman, Camille. You don't have to protect her. Especially not from me."

"I *especially* need to protect her from you."

Two hours and about six glasses of champagne later Tia was draped over a lounge chair in one of the back rooms of Camille's house. She'd made her rounds speaking to reporters and buyers making sure they all knew that she was wearing a CK Davis exclusive, taken pictures, smiled non-stop and modeled back and forth through the large living and dining rooms.

Her head pounded and her feet hurt. She was exhausted and she was afraid. About a half hour ago she'd stopped looking at the clock. She knew the time was ticking down. That's why she'd searched out a place to be alone. If she were going to have a breakdown she didn't need any of the press seeing it. Hell, she didn't need any of the Donovans seeing it.

So for the past fifteen minutes she'd been sitting here in the dark, trying to get her brain out of its champagne-induced haze so she could drive herself back to her apartment. There she could fall flat on her face and let the grief claim her the way it begged to.

She was almost ready to get up when a stream of light invaded her sacred darkness. With an inhale of an intoxicatingly masculine cologne she knew her night had just taken another turn for the worse.

"Hiding out?" Trent asked as he closed the door and switched on a lamp.

Tia pressed her palms into her eyes, praying that when she moved them the pinpricks against her lids would cease. "I'm trying to be alone, if you don't mind."

"I'm looking for some company," he said slowly. "If you don't mind."

Furious at his audacity Tia pulled her hands away from her face and gasped when she realized he was standing directly over her. "Yes. I mind. I'm sure you can find someone to keep you company out there. Lord knows there are plenty of women dying to catch your attention."

"Jealous?" he asked in that cool yet firm voice of his.

"Hell, no! If they want to make fools of themselves for you, they are more than welcome."

Even though she expected him to, Trent didn't respond. He only watched her as if he were seeing something nobody else did. She turned away from him, only to have him grab her chin and turn her back to face him.

"Are you okay?"

"I will be if you'd leave."

"You look sick."

"I am. Sick and tired of being harassed by you."

"You're drunk," he stated flatly.

"I am not."

"I'll take you home."

"I didn't ask you to."

And before she could say another word he was scooping her up off the chair. His strong arms cradled her against his chest.

Why did it have to feel so good? In the midst of all that was bad in her life, why did the touch of this man feel so damn good?

"I don't need you," she said in a small voice trying to hold her head up and not scream against the building pain.

He stopped walking at her words, peering down at her with an indescribable expression. Oh no, it was describable all right. It was a mixture of hunger and danger—a deadly mix, she knew, where Trent Donovan was concerned.

She opened her mouth to tell him to put her down, that she would get Adam or someone else to take her home. But the words died in her throat as his lips touched hers. Heat speared through her body at the contact.

This was no sweet just-get-to-know-you kiss. It was fierce, hot, demanding, stealing. Taking from her all that she'd had pent up for days, no months, or more like years.

She hated kissing. It was too intimate, touching parts of her she'd rather keep reserved. But again, this was no normal kiss. It was a fierce, blistering request—no, demand. Its lustful intent was clear and swept through her senses in deep, flowing waves.

For months, since the night she'd first met him, Tia had dreamed of this, imagining how good it would feel and knowing how easy it would be to fall for this man. And as difficult as it had been, she'd kept her resolve, had refused to call him, to accept the attraction that had sizzled between them since that first touch of hands on the runway.

Now she was powerless, not just because of the amount of champagne she'd ingested, but because as long as his hands were on her, his lips, his tongue, she had no choice but to acquiesce.

His tongue pressed past her teeth searching for hers and claiming it with an arrogant swipe. Hungry and what felt like enraged, he took her mouth, deepening the kiss until all Tia could taste or even think was Trent Donovan.

Chapter 4

Trent turned his black Hummer H3 Alpha onto Redwood Street heading toward the apartment complex Tia had told him she lived in. She was in the passenger seat that he'd reclined for her just before strapping her in. Her eyes were closed and every now and then she would moan, causing him concern over whether she was in pain or whether the champagne was taking its toll and she was about to vomit. The latter wasn't going to be a good thing, especially not in his new truck.

Still he couldn't help again admiring her beauty. It wasn't such a shock to him since her profession was dependent on her looks. But there was something simple and untouched about her smooth skin, high cheekbones and long eyelashes. As she lay with her eyes closed, not speaking, not fighting with him, he was touched by a rarely-seen innocence.

Pulling into the complex Trent frowned. The Sahara West Apartments located just within the Vegas city limits was not a bad complex. Actually, it was a rather nice one, but Tia was making enough money that she clearly could have done better. He parked and went around to the passenger side, opening the door for her.

She hadn't moved so he undid her seat belt and was bending over to lift her once more into his arms when she stirred.

"You don't have to keep carrying me. I can walk," she said slowly.

She was attempting to open her eyes, which didn't look like an easy feat. Yet her speech wasn't slurred. Trent was beginning to think that something else was bothering her, that this wasn't just a result of too much champagne.

"I like the feel of you in my arms," he said as he lifted her out of the truck. The words came out sincerely, intentionally. Trent was a man who knew what he wanted and didn't hesitate going for it. His actions all had a purpose that he carefully worked out in his mind ahead of time.

So when she cuddled against him while he used his hip to close the door he knew the words had done what they were supposed to.

At the door of her apartment he put her down, slowly propping her against the wall. His hands lingered on her hips just to make sure she was steady. And she was, but still he didn't move his hands. He liked touching her. She smelled good, too, like brown sugar and honey.

Her eyes opened easily as she looked up at him. Trent brushed his lips lightly over hers. She kept her eyes on him as if she wanted him to know that she was fully aware of what he was doing.

Struck by a swift slice of guilt at taking advantage of a

woman when she wasn't completely herself, Trent stepped away. "Where's your key?"

Tia didn't speak but reached into her small purse and retrieved the key. She tried to step around him to get to the door but he lifted the key from her hand slipping it into the door and pushing it open. Stepping to the side he let her enter first, then followed and closed the door behind them.

She switched on a lamp that shed only a small amount of light. The living room area was actually small but appeared spacious since she had only a couch, a glass coffee table and a big-screen television on the wall opposite the patio door. In a corner to the left was what Trent assumed was her dining room. There was a counter-height table and two chairs. To say that her furnishings were sparse was an understatement.

"Thank you for seeing me home," she said in a quiet voice.

She'd crossed the room to sit on the couch. Trent hadn't even known she'd moved she'd been so quiet and he'd been so absorbed in checking out her place. "No problem."

In the dim light she looked frail and tired. He moved toward the couch intending to simply see that she was okay and say good-night. But once he was that close to her he couldn't resist. He sat down next to her taking her hand in his. "Are you sure you're all right, Tia?"

She nodded then looked away from him quickly. That was a definite sign that she was *not* okay. It was also a sign for Trent to get the hell out of there. He didn't do pity parties and he definitely didn't do emotional females. If she had something going on that was outside of being intoxicated or that didn't require him to hunt down and possibly shoot someone, he couldn't help.

"Is there someone you'd like me to call?" he asked already moving away from her.

"No," she whispered. "There's no one who can fix this."

Yeah, that was his cue if he'd ever had one. "Okay. Well, I'll leave you alone."

He was about to stand up when she grabbed his wrist and said, "No. Please stay."

In his lifetime Trent had heard more than his share of women saying those exact words. But none of them caused his chest to tighten the way Tia's did. There was something in her eyes, an almost desperation that didn't match her usual snippy attitude.

He sat back in the chair. "Do you want to talk about it?" he asked, knowing he didn't want to hear about whatever it was that had her looking so shaky—especially if it was about another man.

Trent didn't normally consider himself the jealous type. There were more than enough women in this world for all the men to have their share. So he definitely wasn't one to hate another man for having a fine woman on his arm. But he'd be lying if he said the idea of Tia with some another guy didn't rub him the wrong way.

"No. I don't want to talk," she said letting her hand rest on his thigh.

It was wrong, Tia knew. But in less than fifteen minutes it would be midnight. The exact time two years ago that Jake had been bleeding beside her, Jessica dying inside of her.

However, this year she wasn't alone. Trent had brought her home. He'd walked her inside and he was still here. She didn't have to be alone if she didn't choose to be. She could be with Trent and this pain wouldn't seem so bad. He wanted her; he'd made that no secret. So why couldn't she have him? Just for this one night?

Taking another deep breath she inched her hand up his thigh, closer to his groin, and leaned into him. "Do you really want to leave me, Trent?"

He hesitated and for a moment she was afraid he was going to say yes. Instead his hand covered hers on his thigh. "I don't want to take advantage of you."

Tia broke eye contact because the longer he stared at her the guiltier she felt. She leaned closer kissing his neck. "I'm not drunk if that's what you think."

His hand tightened on hers but he didn't push her away. That was a good sign.

"You're not drunk but you're definitely not yourself."

God, he smelled good, strong and virile, if that had a scent. She inhaled deeply, then let her tongue slide along the line of his neck. "I'm tired of being myself," she said.

And that was the God's honest truth. Tia was so tired of being about business, of getting up every day, moving along as if she hadn't a care in the world, when inside she was falling apart.

Trent said she felt good in his arms; well, it had felt good to be in his arms. *Damn good.* And she wanted to hold on to that feeling, at least for tonight. As if he'd read her mind he shifted, wrapping his free arm around her waist, pulling her closer.

"What do you want, Tia?" he asked in a voice that she was sure had grown hoarse.

Tia stopped kissing his neck. Her heart hammered against her chest. With the hand that had accompanied hers on his knee Trent grabbed her chin, tilting her head until he could once again look into her eyes.

"Tell me what you want from me. Because I'm not going to do anything that you aren't completely on board with. Do you understand what I'm saying?"

She did. He wanted her to be sure that she knew whom she was with and what she was doing with him.

Tia didn't have a doubt in her mind.

She was with Trent Donovan. The man that had driven her crazy with lustful thoughts these past few months and scared her witless with his intensity. She wanted him to make love to her tonight, to wash away the painful memories and to satisfy her quaking need.

"I want you in my bed, tonight," she said without further hesitation. "Do *you* understand what *I'm* saying?"

He stood then, picking her up so that her legs wrapped around his waist. His lips crashed down over hers, his tongue plundering hers with deep thrusts and smooth strokes. His hands cupped her bottom, gripping each mound with the promise of more to come. Tia instinctively wrapped her arms around his neck pressing her aching center into him, wanting more, needing it all.

She felt him move, turn in the opposite direction, but his hands were now pushing her dress up farther until he touched the bare flesh of her bottom, skimming the thin wisp of her thong. Her entire body shivered at the brief contact, she sighed and nipped his bottom lip.

"Which way?" he rasped.

Tia couldn't speak but pointed toward the bedroom.

Trent's mind roared with lustful thoughts of how he would take her, claim her, make her his for tonight. He'd thought of this often, each time changing their positions, their words. He wanted her with a desperation he'd never felt before and was more than excited at the notion that he was about to have her. Finally.

She'd unwrapped those sinfully long legs from around him the minute they were in her bedroom. Pushing the straps of her dress down she'd stood still as it fell to the floor. His mouth had literally gone dry at the sight of her in nothing but a black thong, garter belt, silk stockings and heels. The dark color only highlighted her light complexion. The sight of her stroked Trent's skin like a whisper over his rigid sex.

"Come here," he commanded and waited while she walked toward him.

Taking both her beautiful breasts in his hands he squeezed and closed his eyes. How many times had he imagined this? The weight of each globe, the texture of each extended nipple grazing his palms. He bent forward massaging each breast until the nipples puckered between his fingers, then licked them one after the other. She grabbed the back of his head, holding him in place and Trent's senses blurred.

If there was one thing he loved, it was a woman who knew what pleased her. Obviously having her breasts licked pleased Tia. So he continued until she was practically begging him for more.

He moved away from her because control was another one of his pet peeves. She'd told him what she wanted and he had every intention of giving it to her, but on his terms.

He'd removed his suit jacket in the truck so his fingers went instantly to the buttons of his shirt. When she reached out to help him, he pushed her hands away. "No."

She'd tilted her head as if she were going to question him, then instead moved her hands over her stomach, up, until she was cupping each breast similarly to how he'd just done.

Trent was so hard at the sight of her touching herself that he had to clench his teeth to keep from yelling out. Methodically he undressed in front of her watching her fingers move over her pretty nipples.

Before tossing his pants Trent removed his wallet, retrieving two condoms. With protection in hand he reached for Tia and was momentarily startled when she moved away. Looking at her in question he watched as she went around to the other side of the bed, sat and attempted to take off her shoes.

"No," he said quickly. "Leave them on."

Trent was on the bed now, dropping the condoms near one pillow and grabbing Tia around the waist pulling her to the center of the mattress.

The look she gave him was defiant and sexy as hell. Was there anything about this woman that didn't turn him on?

She laced her fingers around the back of his head, then pulled him down for a kiss that had his sex jutting forward, leaking with prepleasure.

He'd planned to go slow, to seduce her, to leave his mark. But as her tongue moved inside his mouth that plan was quickly tossed out. Trent reached for one of the condoms, pulled his mouth away from hers long enough to rip it open with his teeth then was about to sheath himself when she took it out of his hand.

"Let me," she said in a voice so sultry Trent swore he was going to have his release at that very moment.

The voice had only been a preamble to the torture. When she grabbed his length between her hands he'd sucked in a breath. She'd looked up at him with those startling alert eyes and had the audacity to smile as she stretched the latex over him.

Her fingers lingered as she licked her lips and Trent had to resist guiding her to pleasure him. Instead he gently pushed her back so that she was resting against the pillows. He lifted her legs up onto his shoulders, positioned himself between her thighs and said, "Hold on."

Chapter 5

Tia did just that, grasping handfuls of the comforter between her fingers as Trent sank his length deeper and deeper inside of her.

Her eyes closed even though she'd wanted to watch him. If she could keep her focus on Trent, on the here and now, the past couldn't hurt her. But as her lids fluttered and finally closed Tia realized the past wasn't hurting her. Sure, her heart was heavy with the weight of what she'd lost two years ago. But her body was also filled with what she had right now.

And what she had was two hundred–plus pounds of gorgeously muscled, virile man who knew just the way to touch her, kiss her, stroke her. Tilting her head back against the pillows she felt her own teeth sinking into her bottom lip as Trent settled himself snugly inside of her.

"Look at me," he commanded.

Her eyes flew open to find his face only inches from hers, his dark eyes boring into her.

"It's just you and me, Tia. Tonight. Just you and me."

His voice was stern and Tia nodded her head, acknowledging what he was saying to her even as he pulled out of her, sinking blissfully back into her heat.

Trent didn't know what was going on in her mind but he'd be damned if she would think of anyone or anything else besides him tonight. If he had to use every ounce of sexual expertise he possessed he would make certain of that.

Leaning forward he kissed the corner of her lip she'd been biting down on, stroking his tongue over the plumped section before sucking it gently into his mouth. She moaned and he circled his hips, pressing her farther into the mattress. Her thighs tightened and clasped around his waist. He was trapped inside of her, not that he was complaining. His mouth was locked with hers, their tongues mating the same way as their sex.

That's when he felt it. The first inkling of something different. Yes, this was Tia St. Claire he was making love to. And, yes, he'd already adjusted his mind to the fact that for some odd reason she was different from the other women he'd known. But this feeling, circling and swirling in his chest as he moved over her wasn't explainable. And what Trent couldn't explain he either ignored or pounded until his understanding was clear.

At this moment he didn't feel like doing, either.

Instead he tore his mouth away from hers, then reached behind to uncurl her legs. Hooking the backs of each of her knees in the crook of his arms, he lifted them higher, until only the upper half of her body was on the bed. With quick thrusts he moved inside of her watching the sensual play of emotions on her face.

She was gorgeous, her small braids spread across the pillow like a golden halo. Her eyes were half closed, but the hazel orbs shone brightly with desire. Her lips were parted as she panted, lifting her hips to match his rhythm. As lovers went, Tia was scoring more than average marks with him. She matched his intensity and desire every step of the way, challenging him with a look, a shift of her hips, a touch of her hands.

Dammit, that feeling in his chest seemed to magnify with this position. He stopped mid-stroke, closing his eyes in an attempt to get his thoughts together.

And she reacted.

Lifting up from the bed she managed to slip her legs out of his grip so that she was sitting and he was kneeling. Her hands flattened on his chest and she applied pressure as if to tell him to lay down. Trent's eyes opened, finding hers glaring at him in challenge.

"My turn," she said before stroking her tongue over his lips.

Every sane thought ran directly to his erection, making it harder, more determined than ever to find its release. He was lying back now, without a word, smiling up at her as she situated herself above him. Her long legs held her steady as she gripped his sex leading him to her waiting cove. She lowered herself ever so slowly, taking in one excruciating inch at a time. Her braids cascaded over her shoulders in a sexy curtain. Trent lifted his hands grasping handfuls of her hair pushing it back from her face.

Her features were concentrated as she lowered farther and when their bodies touched and he was completely impaled in her she looked at him. "Ready?" she asked.

Trent shifted his hips, settling himself, then grinned. "Ready and waiting. Show me what you've got."

And that she did. With what seemed to be choreo-graphed movements she rotated her hips, lifted slightly upward, then came down over him repeatedly. Trent's mind had gone blank several times as his fingers gripped her hips. With her head thrown back, her breasts jutting forward and moans slipping from her lips Tia rode him like a woman possessed.

Or a woman trying desperately to lose herself in the moment.

Trent continued to watch her, taking her movements and matching them with his own. When she stiffened above him he lifted up from the bed, driving his sex deeper into her while wrapping his arms securely around her back. When her release came she went limp in his arms, her forehead falling forward to rest on his shoulder.

Continuing to work himself inside of her, Trent found his own explosive relief and groaned as her fingernails pressed into the skin of his shoulders. They sat there a moment, both of them trying to catch their breath. Then she shifted, trying to get free of his grasp but he held firm.

"I have to go to the bathroom," she said in a slightly irri-tated voice that just about shattered any thoughts of intimacy.

Trent released her because, after all, he wasn't the cuddling sort of guy. The room grew instantly chilly as she slipped away from him and walked unashamedly naked across the floor to the bathroom. With a sigh Trent lay back on the bed wondering what the hell had just happened.

They'd had sex, that part he knew, and felt, as his breath-ing was just getting back to normal. But he was no fool. In fact, he was smarter than most people gave him credit for. Still, he admitted that it wouldn't take a rocket scientist to know that something wasn't totally right about what had just happened.

When Tia came back into the room Trent had already pulled the comforter and sheets down. He stood as she approached the bed, put her hair up and slipped on a nightgown, lifting her feet as she sat on the end, then he tucked her in, but that didn't matter. He'd seen her gorgeous body naked. Now, no matter what she wore, he'd always have that picture emblazoned in his mind, just the way he liked it.

He was about to move away when she grabbed his wrist. "Are you leaving?" she asked.

Trent couldn't help but frown. This woman was a bundle of contradictions. One minute she was feisty and telling him to get lost, the next she was cuddling in his arms and feeling on him seductively. She'd moaned and just about broke the skin on his back when she came then bit his head off when he tried to hold on to her afterwards. What the hell was up with that?

"I'm going to the bathroom," he said when he should have told her yes he was leaving because he was getting tired of the Dr. Jekyll and Mr. Hyde act.

But as he moved into the bathroom Trent had a sinking suspicion that Tia had needed him tonight. Not "him" specifically but someone. She didn't want to be alone—of that he was certain—and he wasn't complaining about being the one to end up in bed with her.

Still he wondered as he wiped the warm washcloth over his face and down his chest, what was really going on with her.

Tia stepped onto the treadmill the next morning with one goal in mind: walk until her mind was completely clear. Of the anniversary. Of Jake and Jessica. And definitely of Trent Donovan.

When she'd left her apartment well before the crack of

dawn this morning he'd been still asleep in her bed. He'd stayed with her all night, cradling her in his arms as if she were the most important thing in the world to him.

Which she knew was an out-and-out lie.

Trent Donovan didn't give a rat's ass about her. He'd wanted to sleep with her for months now and she'd given him that chance. In fact, he'd done her just as much of a favor by staying. She hadn't wanted to be alone and if she'd had to choose a way to spend that most horrible night, she wasn't about to complain about it being in Trent's arms.

So she swiped at the sweat already beginning to bead on her forehead, pressed the button and walked a little faster. She had been in such a hurry to get out of her apartment without waking Trent that she'd forgotten her iPod so she had nothing else to occupy her mind. Not that music would have helped.

It was the morning after and instead of being curled up in her bed sobbing or even curled up in her bed with the mesmerizing Trent Donovan, she was here at the gym. She was losing her mind, that's exactly what she was doing. Any other woman would be back at her apartment probably gearing up for another round of the most spine-tingling sex she'd ever experienced. But, no, not Tia.

It wasn't worth it. He'd been there when she needed him and that was that. For all she cared Trent Donovan could move on to his next victim and she wouldn't bat an eyelid.

From her bag on the floor Tia's cell phone chirped. She did a running jump and leapt from the treadmill, almost tripping over the bag as she dug her hand inside to find the phone. Looking at the display, she rolled her eyes when she recognized the number.

"Hi, Camille," she said as cheerfully and out of breath

as possible. So much for not being pressed about Trent Donovan, she thought acknowledging her own disappointment that it wasn't him calling.

"Thank God," Camille sighed on the other end. "Where are you? I was so worried when you disappeared from the party last night. When you didn't answer your home phone the ten times I called first thing this morning I began to panic."

With one hand Tia reached into her bag for her towel. Wiping her forehead she cradled the cell phone between her ear and her shoulder. "Sorry. I should have told you I was leaving." *And I probably would have if your soon-to-be brother-in-law hadn't carried me out the back door.* As if he were rescuing her, Tia thought whimsically. Get real, she was not Camille and fairy tales were not on her agenda.

"What's up? I didn't have a shoot today, did I?" Tia was very professional, she kept an accurate schedule and regarded her date book like the Holy Bible.

"No. Nothing work related. I just wanted to make sure you were okay and to ask if you'd like to have lunch."

"Ah, actually, I've got some errands to run today, Camille. So I'm going to have to pass."

"Okay, well, if you change your mind just give me a call on my cell or come on over to the Donovan family estate around one. You remember where that is, right?"

Tia closed her eyes. Camille was just too nice to curse out. She wanted to be alone today, not at some family function for a family that didn't belong to her. "Yes, I remember where it is." They'd done a shoot at the swimming pool there a few weeks ago because Camille thought the intricate shape of the pool—it was shaped like the African continent and painted at the bottom to resemble the tribe that Henry Donovan descended from—would be a lovely backdrop for her Afrocentric collection. "But I really don't think I'll be able to make it."

"That's fine. But, Tia, I hope you're not spending the day alone. You spend far too much time by yourself. You need to get out more."

That wasn't what Tia needed but she couldn't very well tell Camille that. "I like being by myself," she said instead.

Camille was quiet for a moment. "That used to work for me, too."

Tia knew this was where the conversation would shift. Camille would go into how rough a time she'd had it when she was young and with her low self-esteem, thinking that Tia could relate to her. Which she could not since Tia never had self-esteem issues. What she had was a hardened resolve to never be hurt on the level she once was. The loss of a mate was one thing, but the loss of a child at the same time was something completely different.

Just the thought was sometimes unbearable for her. Her grief had festered, she knew. It was unhealthy as the psychiatrist she'd seen immediately after the accident had advised. But Tia didn't give a damn. She'd developed a way to cope and that's what she was doing. All work and no attachments. And she didn't need her employer telling her any differently.

"Listen, Camille, I was in the middle of my workout. Thanks for checking up on me but I'm fine. I'll talk to you on Monday," she said, then disconnected before Camille could say another word. Because Tia was close to breaking down. If Camille had said another word about being alone Tia didn't know that she could hold it in.

Being alone used to work for her, that's what Camille had said. Well, it had worked just fine for Tia for almost two years. But if truth were told, these last two months had been different. Harder, it seemed, because there was a longing inside of her that did not want to be ignored. A longing that Tia feared would be her ultimate demise.

Chapter 6

He wasn't upset.

He was pissed off!

Trent slammed the door of his truck and took long, angry strides towards the door to Madge's Gym. The second the front door closed he'd bolted up in Tia's bed. She hadn't slammed the door. No, she'd closed it as quietly as she could manage. She'd probably forgotten that her alarm system beeped at the opening and closing of any doors with access in and out of the house. It was a good system, he'd noted when he'd seen the control panel near her front door last night.

She'd snuck out on him, the little minx. He thought she'd at least leave him a note, after all he was sleeping in her bed. But there was nothing. That was what pissed him off. It was rude not to say anything the morning after. *And you would know because you do it all the time.*

That was his brother Linc speaking, so Trent ignored that thought. But what he didn't plan to ignore was the fact that she'd begged him to stay with her, then she'd run out. It had only taken one phone call to Joshua Landy, his SEAL teammate, to trace Tia's license tag. Fifteen minutes later he'd received a call with the address to where the car was located. Thank God her car had a built-in GPS locator. Technology was an amazing tool if utilized correctly.

After swinging past his condo to shower and change clothes he quickly made his way to the gym to confront Ms. St. Claire.

It took him less than ten minutes to find her even though the club was crowded on a Sunday morning. She was straddling a bench, her long muscled legs tensing as she worked her upper body on an arm-press weight machine. Instinctively his eyes roamed her body, from her legs to her thighs, to the center he now knew to be hot and wet, and upward to her slim waistline and full breasts. It was there his gaze stopped, hesitated, then went red.

She was using the cable crossover but whatever her weights were they must have been a test to her usual strength because standing entirely too close to her was a Mr. Universe wannabe with long dreadlocked hair and a face that looked all too happy to be touching Tia's arms.

Each time she pulled her arms in, Mr. Universe's hands slid along the length from her shoulder to her wrist. When she expanded outwardly Mr. Universe opened his arms to do the same. The man was straddling the bench, as well, standing so close to Tia that they could actually kiss… That probably wasn't the best scenario to pop into Trent's mind because in no time he was moving across the room to approach them.

"Mornin'," he said in a less than happy tone once he was close enough to them.

Mr. Universe looked over his shoulder. "What's up? You need a trainer for the day? Check the board to see who's not already assigned."

At his sides Trent's fists clenched. Did he look like he needed a personal trainer? His body was in perfect shape courtesy of the U.S. Navy and his current regimen that he'd learned in basic training. Nobody at Madge's Gym could do what he did to keep his body up and he didn't want them to. He also didn't want them doing anything to Tia's body.

"Trent? What are you doing here?" she asked with an accusatory tone that Trent ignored.

"I could ask you the same thing," he replied tartly.

"And the answer would be obvious." She lifted a brow then nodded at Mr. Universe who again touched her arms as she pulled the weights inward.

This guy must have a death wish, Trent thought. That was perfectly fine with him, he hadn't had good hand-to-hand combat in quite some time. Then it hit him that they were in a room full of other people trying to get their workout on. Trent, being one of the infamous Triple Threat Donovans, did not want any more attention than was absolutely necessary. So he reined in his temper as best as he could, and said, "I'd like to speak with you alone, Tia."

Her arms jerked backward and the weights slammed down to the ground. Mr. Universe turned to him with a definite scowl.

"Look, man, she's only got ten more reps to go then you can say whatever it is you need to say to her. But for right now you need to back off."

Trent felt the tension and welcomed the rage, taking a step closer to Mr. Universe and grabbing him by the back of his muscled neck. "I'm not your man. And if anybody's going to be backing off, for your sake and for the sake of the other people in this gym trying to go about their business, it better be you."

Tia was trying to stand but her legs were tangled between the bench, Mr. Universe and now Trent, who were standing so close they could probably smell her. Instead she reached out grabbing Trent's wrist that was squeezing the pulse out of Mr. Universe. The man had tilted his head back to lessen the grip but was unsuccessful. Trent was trained to kill even though he was only trying to intimidate this go-around.

"Let him go, Trent. We can go someplace quiet and talk," she said desperately.

"I don't see your trainer backing off," Trent spat.

"It's okay, Carlo. I'm just going to go and talk to him. I'll finish my workout later."

So Mr. Universe's name was Carlo. Well, Trent didn't give a damn. His name needed to be Mr. Two-Step because that's what he needed to do to get the hell away from Tia, now!

Tia applied pressure to Trent's wrist, trying to pull him off the trainer's neck. "Trent. Stop it. You're making a scene."

"I told him to back off."

"And he will once you let him go."

There was logic to that, Trent thought, but there was also logic to breaking this fool in half for daring to touch Tia. But that was going too far, he knew. So with a deep breath he loosened his grip and took a step back.

Mr. Universe almost tripped over the weight bench trying to get away from him.

"Call another trainer when you're ready, Tia," he said and made a hasty retreat.

Trent couldn't help but smile inwardly. If anybody was going to shape and mold Tia's body it was going to be him.

"Wipe that satisfied smirk off your face. Your performance was juvenile and unnecessary." Tia headed out of the room.

He followed her. "And so was your little exit this morning."

"I don't owe you any explanations," she said over her shoulder, then pushed through the door marked "Stairs."

Trent followed through the door, then reached out grabbing her and pushing her back against the wall. "You owed me at least a goodbye or good riddance. Let's not forget you were the one who set the ball in motion last night. So don't play the wounded victim now."

Even sweating she smelled sexy, like wild berries and musk. It was scintillating, the scent reaching his nostrils then floating through his body like an aphrodisiac. They were alone in this stairwell but the building was full of people. Still he wanted to wrap her legs around his waist and take her right here, right now.

"Nobody said I was a victim," she said pushing against his chest futilely. "I just had things to do."

"And you couldn't wake me up to tell me that. Why sneak out of your own apartment? If you didn't want me there all you had to do was tell me to leave."

She stared at him a moment as if she were going to say something, then she looked away.

"So that's it? You're just going to run away now? I thought you were better than that," Trent said.

"You don't know me," she spat, then took advantage of his shock and twisted out of his reach.

Trent sighed, staring at her as she turned away from him. This was the other side of Tia St. Claire, the side that kept poking its way to the surface only to be pushed back by the wall she'd created around herself. The side that he warned himself to steer clear of.

Trent had never been one to listen, not even to himself.

"I'd like to get to know you," he heard himself saying. She was shaking her head when he approached her again. His hands instantly went around her waist because not touching her wasn't an option. Pulling her back against him Trent nuzzled his face in the crook of her neck.

"We started backwards. I was supposed to take you to dinner and then seduce you."

She chuckled and Trent felt a wave of relief wash over him.

"This isn't a storybook romance," she said finally.

"Who needs romance? I'm talking about eating. If you're going to be the workout queen we have to keep you fed."

She laughed again and Trent felt her relaxing in his arms. What was it that made her so tense and almost afraid at times?

"Look, Trent, we don't have to do this. I'll apologize for skipping out on you this morning. You can apologize for acting like a Neanderthal back there with Carlo and we can both go on about our business."

She'd twisted in his embrace so that they now faced each other and Trent saw that the wall was back in place. She'd gathered her strength and was now facing him as she faced the rest of the world. Only, unlike the rest of the world, Trent knew it was an act. The question was why?

"I'm not apologizing to Mr. Universe. He should know where to put his hands. But I will accept your apology for this morning and offer dinner as a way of calling a truce. We always seem to be fighting each other when it's obvious that's not how we want to carry things."

"What's obvious is that you weren't satisfied with one night," she said with a hint of surprise. "I have to say that's strange coming from one of the Triple Threat Brothers."

Trent didn't flinch at their name, nor did he try to deny the implications. He'd lived for years knowing that the name and reputation that went along with it had paved the way for him to steer clear of many emotional entanglements. Now he wondered if it would work to prevent him from getting what he wanted most. And he could admit, now that he'd caught up with her and had touched her after making love to her, that he wanted Tia St. Claire like a drunk wanted liquor.

The moment she'd seen Trent her heart rate escalated. Tia tried to keep her breathing as neutral as possible as Carlo guided her movements and from the corner of her eye she saw Trent approaching.

Vegas wasn't that big of a town that they couldn't co-incidentally like early Sunday morning workouts at the same gym. And Trent was in excellent condition. Of course he worked out. It had taken about five seconds for her to toss that theory right out the door. And another five seconds for Trent to approach looking like a tall, dark warrior with a purpose. To kill.

Carlo was built and looked like he could possibly survive a round or two before Trent would eventually beat him down but Tia wasn't willing to risk it. She'd defused the situation the best way she knew how. She agreed to talk to Trent alone. But the moment Carlo left, the familiar fear of Trent Donovan had risen, clogging her throat so that words were difficult to come. Her best defense was to run, in the most dignified way possible, of course.

Damn him, he'd followed her. A small part of her knew that he would. Trent was not a man to give up when he wanted something. That was a fact she'd already learned about him.

How foolish of her was it to go into the stairwell? The answer was resoundingly clear as she was now facing the wall, his hands around her waist, his lips on her neck. She could scream from wanting this man so badly. But it wouldn't do her much good.

Logic and past heartache told her to run, to forget appearances and get the hell out of Dodge. Yet something else held her still. A small part of her wanted his touch, his admission to wanting her easing an ache that had occupied her heart for much too long. But Trent wasn't looking to touch her heart. He wanted her body. Another fact made perfectly clear by the thick erection pressing into her bottom.

This she could do, Tia thought with relief. Unlike most women sex for her wasn't a key to her heart. It was as natural and instinctive as breathing. She and Trent were attracted to each other and for once she'd agree that he was correct, there was no use in either of them trying to deny the obvious. So why not continue to sleep with him? As long as they kept it just sex. It would be nice to feel a warm body next to hers on the regular.

"I know you're not afraid of me, Tia," he was saying, his large palms splaying over the exposed skin of her stomach.

"No," she whispered resting her forehead on the wall. "I'm not afraid of you, Trent."

"Then stop trying to run from me." His words were punctuated by one hand slipping beneath the rim of her shorts and the other headed north to cup her already aching breast. Again he'd pressed the thick bulge of his arousal into her bottom as if he would enter her right now if not for the barrier of their clothing.

That thought had Tia's heart pounding, her mouth and center growing moist. She couldn't run now even if she wanted to. As his palm moved farther south cupping her mound, she hissed and arched back into his arms.

"It's like instant fire between us. From that day on the runway when I simply touched your hand I've been craving you."

His voice was hoarse with desire, both his hands working their magic on her until the mere thought of defying this desire between them was out of the question.

"I know," she whispered, then licked her lips.

Trent had been running his tongue alluringly over the line of her neck, but the moment she moistened her lips seemed like his open invitation. With a nudge of his shoulder her head was turning so that claiming her mouth was inevitable.

And with lightning fast strokes his tongue entered her mouth, taking hers on an endless ride of passion, stoking this undeniable fire he'd mentioned between them.

No, denying it was useless, so instead she fell right in line with Trent's intentions, lifting a hand to cup the back of his head, pulling him closer, deeper into the kiss. That action earned a deep growl from Trent as his fingers splayed over her mound, one devious digit parting her moist lips, finding her tightened bud. Over and over the pad of his finger worked the puckered flesh until Tia's knees were growing weak, her breath coming in quick, hot pants.

"Trent," she sighed when his mouth had moved from hers to nip at her chin.

"I know, baby. I know," he said stepping back far enough to turn her around to face him.

It took ten seconds, maybe less for him to maneuver one of her legs out of her shorts. Simultaneously Tia's hands were at the rim of the astoundingly sexy running pants he wore, pushing them down to his muscled thighs. Through the slit in his boxers she found what she needed so desperately, wrapping her greedy fingers around his erection instantly.

"Yes," he moaned, then lifted her free leg to wrap around his waist.

His lips were on hers, hot and demanding as she fondled him, rubbing her fingers over the tight tip of his arousal then stroking downward.

"That's right," he mumbled, "take what you want."

And that she did. When stroking him was no longer enough, her body so hot and eager to take him totally, Tia guided his rigid sex to her weeping center, flexing her hips to take him in. Trent followed her lead by pushing the thin wisp of her thong aside and thrusting so that he filled her in one quick movement.

She threw her head back until it gently hit the wall and she sighed. Trent's forehead dropped to her shoulder as they both kept completely still for a second…two…then three.

Her entire body was trembling, her muscles clenching around his arousal as if to hold on to him forever. Her nails dug into his shoulder and Tia prayed for strength, for oxygen, for anything to keep this moment from ending. Never had she desired a man like this, needed his touch, to keep her mind focused. She'd known it would be this way between them and, truth be told, had been afraid of it. Trent was right, it had happened that first day at the fashion show. The moment she stepped up on the stage and he'd taken her hand, the sparks had begun to fly.

She'd avoided his phone calls for just this reason. Trent Donovan was a powerful man. Not just in his military training or his hefty bank account, but in his allure over women. Surrounding him was this aura of masculinity that was like an aphrodisiac to any woman with a pulse. And she had been no exception.

He began to move inside her, thrusting his hips so that those sexy hollows in his buttocks were pronounced. Yes, in addition to his mouthwatering looks, Trent had a butt that male models would die for. She'd spied it last night and now moved her hands down his strong back to cup them in her hands. He was hard everywhere, tight and tempting and for the moment, all hers.

Chapter 7

Trent couldn't believe this. He was not taking her in a stairwell. It couldn't be.

He was a grown man. He was educated and privileged and dammit, he had a house with a huge bed. So why did he have this woman plastered to this wall, pounding into her like a horny high schooler ready to scream with the powerful release he could feel building in the base of his spine?

Because she was Tia St. Claire.

And he loved being inside of her. The two times he'd taken her last night had hardly been enough. This had to be the fastest growing addiction on record. One night and he couldn't get enough. Even now, as his length moved in and out of her, coated with her sweet honey, clenched by her tightening muscles, he wanted more.

She held his buttocks firm in her hands, pushing him in deeper, holding him steady as he pulled out, whispering in his ear as he sank back in.

"Yes, Trent. More."

The words were a sweet melody in his ear. Not that he hadn't heard them before, but all the other female voices that had bounced around in his head over the years had mysteriously disappeared. There was only one voice now, one woman.

He gave her what she asked for, lifting her other leg and crossing her legs behind his back. Now cupping her buttocks Trent drove into her with his intense desire. Her head fell back, her mouth open as she panted and moaned. He licked her neck, loving the honey-toned skin. Her breasts were bound in the fitted sports bra she wore but he had only to close his eyes and he saw them bared, moving and bouncing with the rhythm he'd created.

She was perfect. This moment was perfect. Regardless of where they were, being inside her, about to release into her was absolutely perfect.

Except…

His mind roared with realization. Tia gripped his shoulders, her moans growing louder. He kissed her, trapping the scream of release in his mouth while thrusting once more, feeling his own orgasm tunnel through his body.

For endless moments they stayed that way, his lips on hers, his sex locked securely in hers. Then Trent reluctantly pulled back, resting his forehead against hers as they both struggled to catch their breath.

When he thought his heartbeat was strong enough to sustain normal conversation he said, "I'm sorry."

Her lashes, naturally long and untouched by makeup, fluttered, her lids lifting. She had beautiful eyes, hazel with tiny flecks of green and gold that looked almost feline.

"Sorry? For wha…" she closed her mouth, cursed, then looked away.

Trent felt her begin to tense and gently let her unwrap her legs from around him. When he knew she was stable he took a step back and began fixing his clothes. "I should have protected you," he said as he adjusted his pants. "I've never forgotten before." He cursed himself as she dragged her hands through her hair, then bent forward to fix her shorts.

Stooping down he helped her put her foot back into her shorts then pulled them up her legs. She hadn't seemed to mind him helping her dress but now she stood there, still and unspeaking.

"Tia," he began cupping her face with one hand.

She shook her head. "No. Don't apologize again. We're both adults. I should have said something."

For a moment Trent could only stare at her. Into those magnificent eyes he searched for answers, for reasons why she reacted to things in certain ways, why she said what she said. But it had already begun, she was closing herself off to him once more.

"It won't happen again," he said finally, then leaned in for a soft kiss on her lips.

She nodded but did not kiss him back.

"I really need to get a shower and leave. I have errands to run," she said when he still stood in front of her.

"Right," he said wanting to spend more time with her but knowing it was a mistake. Trent did not spend time with women. He did what was necessary to seduce them and he moved on. He and Tia were not dating, or courting or whatever they called it these days. They were having hot earth-shattering sex.

"I'll walk you to the locker room," he offered moving to the side so she could take the steps beside him.

They took the two flights in silence, then Trent opened the door and let her out into the long hallway that led to the female locker rooms. When they arrived at that door she turned, looking up to him. A few of her braids had escaped the ponytail she wore and he fingered one, loving the soft texture, the beautiful golden color that seemed to enhance her intriguing features.

"I'm okay with this, Trent," she said finally.

"This?" he inquired.

The left side of her mouth lifted slowly, the smile small but just as potent, tugging softly on something in his chest.

"Yeah, this thing between us. I'm okay with having sex with you." The smile grew a little bigger and Trent struggled to breathe. "I actually like it. A lot," she added.

"Good," he said ignoring any foreign emotions that might be trickling through his body at her words. "I like it a lot, too."

She chuckled then and Trent could swear he'd never heard anything as sweet. "I'm glad to hear that."

"So—" his fingers moved from her hair to skate lightly across her jaw "—when do we do it again?"

"Insatiable," she whispered, then stood on tiptoe to run her tongue along his lips. "I like that, too."

He couldn't help it. He tried, he really did. Coming down the steps Trent swore he wasn't going to touch her again, he wasn't going to act like a teenager with his nose wide open. Still, one arm went around her waist, capturing her before she could retreat. He touched her lips again, tentatively at first, watching her watch him. He kissed her again, saw the beginning haze of lust in her eyes and kissed her once more, this time letting his tongue touch hers. An innocent swipe, a pleasurable lick and then the kiss bloomed. It was soft, arousing, intimate, enticing. But the clincher was, it wasn't filled with lust, but some simple thing akin to longing, to need.

Her arms wrapped around his neck and he brought his around her waist. Her body was pressed against his and he kissed her. Simply kissed her. His mind filled neither with desire nor any sexual urgings. Sure, there was some rousing in his pants but it wasn't the urgent emotion he normally felt when kissing a woman. This exchange was starkly different. Trent recognized it and released it just the same.

She pulled away slowly, then took a step away from him. With their gazes locked she backed into the door leading to the locker rooms and whispered, "Soon."

She disappeared through the swinging door before he could utter another word. Which worked just fine for him because for the first time in his life Trent Donovan had been left speechless.

Twenty-four hours. That's how long he'd managed to avoid calling Tia. The last thing Trent wanted was to appear as if he needed her. Which, coincidentally he did.

Getting through the rest of Sunday hadn't been too bad since he'd already had an appointment to play golf with his brothers. Adam was the one trying to get the brothers and their father hooked on the game. Trent personally needed more of a contact sport like football or basketball, but he'd indulge his little brother for a while longer. Besides, it was time the Donovan men spent together.

The evening was a little more difficult since memories of the previous night kept interrupting his thoughts. During those memories, Trent couldn't help but think about the times that Tia had appeared haunted.

Finding her in the dark room at Adam's house had been the first shock. She should have been out mingling, enjoying the party that would undoubtedly lead to even more career prospects for her. Instead she was closed in a room after apparently drinking too many glasses of champagne. And while she had purposely sought solitude, she hadn't wanted to be alone.

That's why she'd invited him in and eventually to stay. Trent had been so focused on getting her into bed that he didn't give himself a lot of time to consider the facts. Tia had been afraid of something that night. And whatever it was, it had scared her so much she'd resorted to being with him, a man she'd previously acted as if she detested.

Trent had always been the inquisitive brother. His habit of investigating any and everything had caused more than one disagreement in his family. But that had never stopped him before.

So first thing Monday morning he had run a complete background check on Tia Marisal St. Claire. The results hadn't been what he'd expected. In fact, it had taken him hours to come to grips with it and the way it made him feel.

He'd wanted to call her that night but couldn't figure what to say to her, especially with his newfound information. However, he needed to talk to somebody to decide what his next move should be. Outside of his brothers and his father the only other person Trent would ever seek out for advice—advice he would actually listen to—would be his mother.

Beverly Donovan was the glue holding the Donovan men together. She was their rock, their strength, the first woman any of them had ever loved. The only woman Trent loved. While to most men their mother was the light of their life, to Trent, Beverly was so much more.

When he'd gone into the Navy he didn't have any girlfriend left at home to write him sappy letters laced with perfume. His brothers were in college and had lives of their own. His father wasn't all that pleased that his son had decided to enter the military but had tried valiantly to respect Trent's wishes. But it was Beverly who had written to Trent weekly. It was she who would wait on the third Sunday of every month at precisely six o'clock in the evening for his phone call. Only she knew of the times he'd doubted himself and how best to kick his butt into gear. She was one of his best friends and the only honest woman he'd ever known.

Late Tuesday afternoon he'd decided to go and see her, to get her take on the information he'd found on Tia.

"She's having a girls' night with Camille, Jade and Noelle. They're talking about that baby shower again," Linc said with a sigh and a shake of his head in answer to Trent's question as to where their mother was. "Man, I'll be so glad when Jade delivers. Don't get me wrong, the most beautiful sight a man could ever see is his wife pregnant with his child. But damn, I can't take these mood swings much longer."

Adam and Henry Donovan laughed as they sat in the pool room at the Donovan estate. Trent had heard them talking and come in, asking where his mother was.

"I can't wait for Camille to get pregnant," Adam said rubbing his hands over his legs. "Camille is going to be a great mother."

"Slow down, son," Henry chuckled. "Enjoy some alone time with your woman first. I tried to tell this one that but he was too fast for me. Once those babies get here, Jade won't remember your name."

Linc looked horrified and Trent couldn't help but chuckle himself. They all looked happy and content, talking about their women and babies and such. Trent felt like an outsider, but then he'd always felt that way. So different from Adam and Linc he'd always been. While they were college and business suited, Trent was more hands-on, physical and dominating.

"So what brings you by, Trent?" Henry asked. "We don't usually see you during the week."

"Yeah, when's your next assignment?" Linc asked as he unhooked his cell phone and looked at it. Probably checking for a call or text message from Jade.

His big brother was so whipped, Trent almost laughed again. "I'm free of assignments for a while."

"After Connecticut you should be taking a hiatus. I heard that was a close call with the explosion and shooting at Bennett Industries, then the arrest of the stalker lady and that lieutenant from the Marines," Adam added.

"I read about that." Henry lifted one of his favorite cigars out of the box and stuck it in his mouth. He would keep it there, unlit for at least fifteen minutes before eventually lighting and smoking it. "Terrible shame. I hope the family's doing okay."

"They are," Trent said. "I spoke to Sam last night."

"Really?" Linc looked up from his phone. "Did you also talk to his sister?"

Trent shook his head. His brothers didn't forget a thing. "No I didn't talk to Lynn because we have nothing else to talk about."

"My boys," Henry shook his head. "Just over a year ago all of you were breaking hearts across the nation. Now only one remains. When are you going to settle down, Trent?"

"I'm not," Trent answered quickly, adamantly.

Adam was first to laugh while Linc went back to whatever he was doing with his cell phone. "He just hasn't been caught yet," Linc mumbled.

"Or has he?" Adam asked, his annoying chuckling

finally ceasing. "Camille was pretty upset when she couldn't find Tia after the party Saturday. She called her house a couple of times but didn't get an answer."

Trent wisely kept his mouth shut.

"Who's Tia?" Henry asked taking his cigar out of his mouth to study it.

"She's the model," Linc chimed in.

"When Camille spoke to her on Sunday she said Tia sounded strange but assured her she was all right."

"So." Trent stood, going to the patio door and opening it. Although it was March, it was almost sixty degrees in Vegas and getting warmer as the topic of conversation was going in a direction Trent didn't want.

The previous topic, his military career and how dangerous it was, wasn't any better. Trent loved his family and didn't like the fact that they worried about him when he was away on assignments. But that was his job, he couldn't really see himself doing anything else.

Or at least he hadn't until Sam had proposed the private investigation agency. The jury was still out on that one.

"So," Adam continued. "One of the drivers told me he saw you carrying Tia to your car before the party was over."

Trent sighed. This town was too damn small. "She wasn't feeling well so I took her home."

"Yeah, you're the perfect gentleman," Linc quipped. "Today's Tuesday—is she able to walk on her own now?"

Adam was laughing again and Trent wanted to stuff something into his big mouth to keep him quiet.

"She was walking yesterday," he answered tightly.

"Then you obviously didn't do your job right," Adam guffawed.

Trent moved across the room taking a seat on one of the bar stools. "Does Camille know you're this vulgar? She gets after me about every word that comes out of my mouth but yet you talk like that."

Adam straightened in the chair still smiling. "I'm smart enough not to talk like this around her."

"Just like Trent's smart enough to see a woman who's in trouble home safely. Good job, son," Henry said.

His father was tracing a finger along the line of his cigar now and Trent wondered when he was just going to smoke the damn thing. Sunday on the golf range had been so nice with them. For a minute Trent had thought Adam was going to mention Tia, but he hadn't. He wondered why he did now.

"Thanks, Dad. I'm glad somebody knows when to do the right thing." He glared at his brothers.

"The right thing?" Linc grinned. "What time did you leave her in the morning and have you called her since?"

Trent didn't answer.

Adam went on, "Well, she worked on a catalog shoot yesterday. I know because I stopped by the shoot to see Camille and Tia was there."

And that's why Adam was bringing her up now. Trent wondered if she'd said anything about him.

"You slept with her, didn't you?" Linc asked as he sat back in his seat, eyeing Trent.

Trent couldn't help but grin. His brothers knew him too well. "What's my name?"

Chapter 8

At Trent's words they all laughed, Henry included, even though he still hadn't lit that cigar.

"Now back to Linc's question. Have you called her?" Adam asked.

Trent sighed. "No." When Adam opened his mouth to speak again Trent held up a hand to stop him. "But not for the reason you think."

"There doesn't have to be a reason, it's just what you do," Linc said seriously.

For a minute Trent was bothered by the tinge of disappointment he heard in Linc's voice. "What's that supposed to mean?"

"It means, you are still in your love 'em and leave 'em stage. You're not calling her because you got what you wanted all along."

With another woman that might have been true. But Trent still wanted Tia, desperately.

"What would you say if I said you were wrong?"

Every Donovan in the room had his gaze aimed at him. To himself even Trent had to admit that the words sounded strange. "I wanted to call her. As soon as I left her on Sunday afternoon I wanted to call."

Linc dropped his cell phone into his lap. Adam sat straight up in his seat. And Henry, who had just lit the lighter and held it to his cigar, watched Trent in shock as the flame quickly tapped out.

"So did you?" Linc finally asked.

"No."

Adam leaned forward, his arms resting on his legs as he continued to stare at Trent. "Why?"

"Because I had her investigated instead."

"What?"

"Now *that* sounds like my brother."

Linc and Adam spoke simultaneously. Henry shook his head, flicked the lighter once more and took his first puff of the cigar.

"I did it because I think she's hiding something and I wanted to know what it was."

"You just slept with her, she doesn't have to divulge her entire life history to you just to have sex," Adam said disgustedly.

"What did you find out?"

Trent knew that Adam would take this personally. Tia and Camille were good friends. Trent was no fool, he knew that whatever went down between him and Tia would directly effect his sister-in-law and ultimately his brother. That was one reason why Trent was determined to do the right thing in this situation. While he usually dealt with women in a callous and cold manner, his family was a different matter entirely. He would do whatever he needed to ensure they weren't hurt or stressed by his actions.

"She's had some pretty hefty emotional baggage with her. I think that's why she was so upset at the party. I took her home because she'd been drinking and I didn't want her to try and drive herself."

"Chivalry's not dead, I see," Henry said between puffs.

His father wasn't doing a lot of talking, but he was listening, Trent knew. That's what Henry did. He listened, he thought and then he talked. If Trent were lucky he'd make it out of here just barely scathed by what his father could possibly say to him in this situation. While the Triple Threat Donovans had their reign Henry Donovan had constantly preached to his sons about loving and respecting women, about finding the right one, settling down and building their own legacy. Trent had no doubt that the same lecture was waiting in the wings for him, yet again.

"Tell us what the report said, Trent," Linc prodded.

Adam shook his head, standing. "I don't want to know."

"Yes, you do," Linc said. "Sit down. He's our brother before she's Camille's friend. Besides, from the way he's looking it might be something we all need to know."

Adam sat reluctantly. "You need to learn how to respect people's privacy," he told Trent.

"There's no such thing as privacy in this day and age," Trent told him. "Besides, I wasn't doing it because I didn't trust her. I did it because I was worried about her."

"Wow. That's new." Linc rubbed a hand across his jaw.

"Look, she was engaged to be married and she was pregnant two years ago."

The men remained silent for a moment.

"So where's the husband and the baby?" Adam finally asked.

"They died," Trent said solemnly.

"How?" Linc sounded nervous.

"They were in a car accident. Her fiancé, Jake Baskins, who was also her manager at the time, was distracted by an oncoming eighteen wheeler. He lost control of the car and drove over an embankment. He died instantly. Tia was knocked out. By the time she arrived at the hospital she was hemorrhaging. The baby, a little girl, died an hour after the crash. She was only two weeks away from delivering."

"Damn." Adam sat back in the chair.

Linc's fingers now visibly shook as he continued to rub his chin.

"That's not all," Trent continued. "The night of the party was the second anniversary of the accident. She'd been drinking because she was hurting." And he'd taken her home and made love to her. For that he felt like the biggest jerk in all civilization.

Yet, a part of him sensed that being with her in that way had helped her through. She'd held on to him so tightly as if she were afraid he'd vanish and she'd be left alone to commemorate the anniversary by herself. He hoped by staying with her he'd saved her from even more pain.

"She did look a little tense that night," Adam said. "I wonder if Camille knows. Of course she doesn't, she would never have insisted that Tia come if she knew what she was going through."

"I get the impression she doesn't talk about her past much."

"So how was she with you that night?" Linc asked. At Trent's raised brow he rephrased his question. "I mean, did she seem upset or high-strung or what?"

"She was definitely a little testy at first. But once we got to her place she was cool until after…" Trent's words trailed off and he cleared his throat. "Then she went from sated to tense to needy all in the span of about fifteen minutes. She asked me not to leave so I didn't."

"Good move," Henry finally chimed in.

The brothers looked his way in question.

"She needed you that night and you were smart enough to realize that," Henry said. "Had you left her, the pain of that anniversary would have been compounded for her. As carefree and unfeeling as you like to portray yourself, I know you wouldn't have wanted that."

His father was right. Trent would have felt miserable if he'd found out later why she wanted him there. Although, in retrospect if he'd known all this about her a month ago, he doubted he would have pursued her this relentlessly.

"So what are you going to do now that you know? You're not going to duck her are you?" Adam asked cautiously.

"I can't duck her if she hasn't called me," he replied a little too quickly.

"Wait a minute, the last time you saw her was Sunday afternoon? It's now Tuesday evening and you haven't heard from her?" Linc stated, a smile spreading across his face.

"Don't even go there," Trent warned. "Adam just said she was working on a catalog shot for Camille. She's not ducking me." Although the thought had crossed his mind.

Adam chuckled. "That would be something, wouldn't it. Trent Donovan finally getting a dose of his own medicine."

Besides Trent, Henry was the only one not laughing. "My advice to you, son, is not to play games with this one. She's had a traumatic time so if you're not sure about where you're heading with her, then steer clear. Some people don't deal well with emotional issues. Your toying with her might lead to something catastrophic and I know you don't want that on your shoulders." Henry took another puff of his cigar, blew smoke into the air and nodded toward Trent. "Think about what you want from her carefully before making another move. I've got a feeling she's not the type you're used to dealing with."

Tia looked at the cheerful yellow, green and white invitation once more and took a deep, steadying breath. She could do this, she told herself over and over again. She had to do this.

About a month ago she'd received the invitation and after contemplating a day or two, she had responded that she would attend. Jade Donovan was a lovely woman who had invited Tia to her spa on more than one occasion to unwind. Her husband Linc was easy to look at and even easier to like. The fact that he was Adam's brother and Camille's future brother-in-law just made liking Linc and Jade all the more easy.

But Trent…now he was another story.

It had been three days since she'd seen or heard from Trent and she was beginning to feel like an addict going through withdrawal. Thinking about him now had her center throbbing. Squeezing her legs together tightly she scooted closer to the desk, focusing her eyes on the computer screen.

The phone rang, interrupting Tia's thoughts. Tia answered; it was her mother. Madeline St. Claire checked up on Tia with regularity. She was so glad Tia went to the party on the painful anniversary instead of sitting at home remembering.

"So how was the party?" Madeline asked.

"The party was fine. Lots of rich people drinking champagne in pretty clothes," she responded in what she hoped was a sufficiently cheerful voice.

"Did you meet anyone?"

Her mother was dying for Tia to get into a new relationship. And no matter how many times Tia told her that wasn't going to happen, Madeline kept on saying it.

"I'm not looking to meet anyone, Mama."

"You are a beautiful woman, Tia. And you're still young. There's no reason why you can't give love another chance."

No reason except for the severely fractured heart she still carried. "I don't want another relationship."

"You can't close yourself off because of what happened. Some things are simply meant to be."

"You mean my fiancé and my child were meant to die?" she'd unintentionally raised her voice.

"No. I mean that God doesn't make mistakes," Madeline said calmly. "Honey, I know you were terribly hurt, but you're still living and there's a reason for that. There's more life for you to live. You've just got to take a step outside and live it."

She didn't know why she said it. Well, yes, she did. She'd heard this speech from her mother too many times to count and she just didn't feel like hearing it anymore. So the words tumbled out of her mouth without another thought. "My boss's brother-in-law brought me home."

"Really?" Madeline's voice perked up. "Is he nice-looking?"

Tia sighed. "That's an understatement."

"Oh. Well, is he single?"

"Happily so."

"Do you like him?"

"Well enough, I guess." She was not about to tell her mother that she was in lust with Mr. Trent Donovan. Even though her mother lived in Phoenix Tia was willing to bet she'd heard of Trent and or his family. Beverly Donovan was world renowned for her work with domestic violence organizations, and Tia's mother volunteered at a local women's shelter. The shelter would have received some of Beverly's generous donations. The legend of the Triple Threat Donovans was known up and down the west coast, thanks to the tabloids.

"So are you going to see him again?"

Now came the dread. Tia realized she'd just traded one touchy subject for another. "We're not dating, Mama. He just brought me home." And stayed the night and sexed me like crazy. Then held me while I trembled from the memories.

"Maybe you should consider dating him. Or some other man to your liking."

Tia came up with an excuse and got off the phone then. Continuing to talk about Trent with her mother was only making matters worse. Nothing serious was going to come of her being with him so there was really no use putting those ideas in Madeline's head.

Bringing her mind back to the matter at hand, Tia once again looked at the computer screen. All last week she'd attempted to go into a baby store to buy a gift for Jade's baby shower. But each time she'd come up to the door she'd stopped. Her heart had raced, her hands shaking and sweating. She couldn't do it.

Before, she'd decorated the prettiest room for Jessica in the softest lavender, yellow and pink. Her crib had been a vanilla-colored cascade with white lace bedding. The carpet mauve, the drapes pink with yellow balloons. And in the corner was a white rocker where she would sit to rock Jessica to sleep. Inhaling deeply, Tia could still smell the distinctive baby scent that filtered through the room. She'd loved to go in there early in the morning, before the sun or Jake had risen. She'd imagine Jessica asleep in the crib as she touched the sheets.

Teardrops fell onto her hand, rolling down her fingers

to land on the black keyboard. Clearing her throat and sitting up straight in the chair, Tia reached for a tissue to clean off her hand and her keyboard, then attempted to focus once more.

Going into a baby store again was out of the question. Thank goodness for the Internet. For the last hour since she'd returned from a fitting with Camille, she'd been perusing Web sites selling baby products.

Jade was having twins. They hadn't found out the sex because, as Camille had told her, Linc wanted to be surprised. So whatever she purchased would have to be unisex.

She found a great gift basket full of all things baby-oriented and was trying to decide between that and a double stroller when there was a knock at her door.

Glancing at the clock she noted it was a little after seven and wondered who could be visiting her at this hour. Other than Camille and Dana, Tia didn't have many social visitors.

Tia peered through the peephole and her breath caught as she saw his chest first—and, man, what a chest; it should be a sin to be as finely built as this man—then his face. It wasn't enough that he played into her one indulgence, physical fitness. No, he had to be fine as hell to boot. She wasn't quite sure if it was the mixture of milk-chocolate-toned skin and dark penetrating eyes or the strong jaw and tempting mouth that made her the hottest. At any rate she was all but drooling with one eye pressed against the door and she felt ridiculous.

Pulling the door open she steadied her breathing and tried for a casual smile. "Hi."

For a few seconds he only stood there, staring at her with that look that made her feel naked no matter how many clothes she wore. Since she had no plans of going out tonight she wore an old Lakers jersey over shorts that were too short to wear outside. Usually being with or without clothes didn't rattle her because as a model she was used to undressing and dressing in front of strangers. But Trent's glare made her nervous.

"Hi, yourself," he said suddenly, then stepped inside, his hands instantly going around her waist as he backed her into the apartment. "Remind me to thank Kobe Bryant later," he said just before his lips landed on hers, stealing the breath she was about to take.

Chapter 9

His tongue stroked hers as if that were its sole purpose. Soft and gentle, then probing and insistent, he moved his lips over hers, all the while his hands slid from her waist to cup her bottom.

Tia heard the door slam, then felt herself being lifted from the floor. Without breaking the kiss she willingly wrapped her legs around his waist, clasping them at the ankles. He moved through the apartment, stopping only when he bumped into the kitchen counter where he placed her.

"I have this same jersey at home," he said in a gruff voice while his fingers went to the edges of the jersey and lifted it upward. "But it doesn't look half as good on me," he finished after he'd removed the jersey.

Now he stared down, then back up to her face with what looked like defeat. "Why do you have this on?" he asked referring to the tank top she wore.

"Huh?" she asked confused and still trying to catch her breath. She barely knew where she was, let alone what he was saying. The last clear memory she had was sitting at the computer looking for a baby shower gift. Now it appeared she was on the kitchen counter, her jersey thrown on the floor and him staring at her quizzically.

"You're wearing too many damned clothes," he complained.

She looked down, then picked up on his meaning and laughed. "I don't usually walk around naked anticipating a man to knock on my door and want sex."

Placing his palms on either side of her on the counter Trent lowered his head and took a deep breath.

"Sorry," he said finally, looking up at her again. "I meant to stop by to say hello and see if you'd eaten dinner yet."

Tilting her head Tia nodded. "Uh-huh."

"Really," he insisted. "I did not come here intending to ravish you."

She arched a brow. "So you don't want sex?"

He grinned, a wide, tooth-filled grin that scraped along the bumpy surface of her heart.

Each time she'd seen Trent he'd had this intense look about him. Even when they'd made love that night he was focused, on her pleasure and his. Never had she seen him happy or relaxed. She was surprised right now, he looked both.

"I didn't say all that."

Because the look was infectious, she smiled, as well. "That's what I thought." Using her hands she pushed herself off the counter then waited for him to back up. Which he didn't so their bodies remained crunched together.

"Um, the answer to your question is no, I haven't eaten yet. Do you plan on feeding me before or after you ravish me?" Because the mere thought of him touching her sounded almost as good as a nice hot meal.

He'd put those hypnotic hands on her again, this time they moved down her outer thighs, around front and back up again until one hand was cupping her juncture and the other was moving steadily to grasp her breast. "Let's order pizza, then head to the bedroom. By the time we're finished with round one the food should be here."

Tia couldn't help but chuckle with excitement. In the two years since Jake's death she'd had sex a couple of times with men that interested her only a little. Those encounters were solely for physical purposes and left her neither happy nor particularly excited to indulge in them again.

With Trent it had been the total opposite. She wanted him to touch her, to kiss her, to carry her off to her bedroom and make love to her again and again. The added bonus that his desire for her was exhilarating only enhanced the anticipated pleasure.

To show that she was game for his suggestion she slipped a hand between them cupping his thick erection in her palm, then leaned forward to nip at his bottom lip. "There are menus in the bottom drawer over there. I like my pizza with extra cheese."

Giving his arousal a teasing squeeze, she moved away from him, taking off her tank top and tossing it in his direction as she left the kitchen.

He wasn't lying. He'd come over to check on her. After his conversation with his father and brothers yesterday Trent had decided that staying away from Tia was not an option.

On the drive over here he'd considered all the information he'd found on her and decided to deal with that as needed. If she didn't bring it up, neither would he. They enjoyed sex with each other. There was no need to complicate that. The fact that she hadn't called him in the last three days, well, he intended to bring that up when he had her where he wanted her.

He'd decided that even though he didn't want any type of committed relationship, going three days without hearing or seeing her wasn't going to work. His body was on overdrive, his sex leading him around with only one destination in mind.

It was with that in mind that Trent hastily moved to the drawer she'd indicated, picked up the phone and placed their order. In minutes he was heading into the bedroom, his clothes coming off as he went.

By the time he'd entered the bedroom he wore only boxers. He stopped the moment he spied her in the center of the bed.

She was naked, gloriously, blessedly naked. Her golden skin highlighted by the dark brown comforter on the bed. The pillows were propped up behind her, one leg lying straight, the other lifted so that her foot was planted flat on the mattress. Her hair was loose, her eyes cast in a sheen of desire as she lifted a finger, beckoning him to come forward.

Trent's mind roared, his erection poking swiftly through the slit in his boxers. He took one step towards her, then turned back, found his pants and retrieved the condoms he'd placed in his wallet. Moving forward he tossed them on the nightstand, keeping one in his hand, then climbed onto the bed.

"What took you so long?" she asked reaching up for him.

"You wanted extra cheese, remember?" He grinned down at her then took her lips. Kissing her was like a burst of sunshine. Each time his lips touched hers his entire body lit up from the inside out. No matter what he had been thinking or feeling, the touch of her lips set off a warm, sensuous feeling in him that Trent was quickly becoming addicted to.

Adjusting himself over her he pushed her back farther then felt her reaching into his hand to take the condom.

"Let's get you suited up first," she said pulling her mouth away from his.

With her hands on his shoulders she pushed him back enough so that she could grab his erection. "You're being awfully bossy today," he said, then followed up with a moan as she stroked his length.

"You came here for food and sex so we might as well get down to business."

She'd released him only to remove the condom from the pack and Trent stilled with her words. They were casual, said with an air of teasing, yet he wasn't quite pleased with them. The thought that this was just a happy-go-lucky sexual encounter didn't sit as comfortably with him as it had on the drive over.

Tia had finished suiting him up and was stroking one hand over his length while her other hand slipped between her legs, touching herself as she touched him. All thought of what type of encounter this was fled from Trent's mind.

His gaze fell to her center watching intently as her fingers grazed over her aroused flesh. Arching her back she moaned, continuing to sweetly torture both of them. Wrapping his hand around her wrist Trent pulled her fingers away from her center, lifting them slowly to his mouth. One at a time and in a motion so slow he could memorize it, he licked the damp digits clean.

She'd watched him, her other hand moving methodically over his erection as she did. Placing her free hand alongside its mate at his groin, Trent touched the smooth center of her, letting his fingers move downward until parting her nether lips was inevitable. She was already open to him, already wet and waiting. His finger slid slowly, sinuously over her aroused flesh and his breath caught.

He'd known the moment he'd first seen her that this was what he wanted to do to her. What he hadn't counted on was how frequently he would want to do it.

"Three days is too long," he whispered.

Her mouth opened slightly, her tongue slipping out to move seductively over her lips. "You could have come sooner," she answered with eyes intent on his.

"Did you want me sooner?"

She lifted her hips silently coaxing his finger to delve deeper. Trent pulled back hovering just above where she wanted him.

Her fingers tightened on his length, one hand slipping back to cup his sac. "I wanted you on the first day."

Trent growled, dipping his finger finally into her waiting center. She arched her back, her sweet walls clenching his finger tightly. "We won't wait this long again," he promised.

"Agreed," she answered pumping with the motions of his hand.

His fingers slipping easily in and out of her was driving Trent insane. Her hand wrapped securely around his arousal pushed him steadily over the edge.

"Enough," he said roughly, removing his hands from her center and moving out of her reach. With a flexing of his hips Trent entered her with a deep stroke. She gasped, then wrapped her legs securely around his waist, settling in for the ride.

And ride her he did, thrusting so deep inside her he would swear they were connected. His eyes closed, the muscles in his shoulders bunching as he worked her. God, she was fantastic. Never in a million years would he have thought he'd enjoy sex this intensely with a woman.

Still, this felt somehow different, more gratifying on so many levels. Tia raised herself up so that they were sitting in the middle of her bed, arms, legs and centers entangled. She now rode while he pumped in conjunction with her movements. It was exhilarating to say the least as they both moaned and kissed. Their hearts beat rapidly, their minds solely focused on each other's mutual pleasure.

Nothing in her file had revealed what a sex goddess she was. There was no hint, no warning that if he touched her he'd become addicted, wanting, no, needing to feel her honeyed walls grasping him on a daily basis. Wanting her sweet lips on his, her tongue tangling with his own more often than not.

For the first time in Trent's life he wasn't prepared, wasn't equipped to deal with the onslaught of desire. And when her legs shivered, her entire body trembling over his, she screamed out his name and he fell.

His mind went blank, but his soul began to fill, with what he couldn't quite explain. His name was a litany on her lips, wrapping around him, cloaking him as he drifted, plunged, then emptied his very essence.

On a ragged moan he pulled her even closer. Her hair draped them both as he rested his head on her chest. Hearing her rapid heartbeat melding with his own, Trent felt the first ebbings of dread and something a Navy SEAL should never encounter, fear.

Strings of gooey cheese stretched from her mouth to the slice of pizza Tia steadily pulled away from her. Breaking it with her fingers she licked her lips and proceeded to chew. The look of pure bliss that covered her face was almost equivalent to the moment when she'd climaxed.

Trent simply watched, completely fascinated by the effect watching her eat was having on him. He'd had dinner with women before, watched them sit across from him and consume anything from a bird-like salad to a whole lobster, but none of that seemed to compare to Tia.

When his breathing had steadied enough so that he could speak coherently he'd lifted her from the bed, carrying her into the shower where they stood under the warm cascade of water. Like two teenagers they'd giggled and played as soapy hands attempted to cleanse each other's body. Only once did Trent give in to the urge and kiss her, long and deep with her back plastered against the cool tiled wall. It was then that she'd pulled away and complained of being hungry.

So they'd gotten out of the shower just minutes before the pizza guy appeared at the door. Now they were sitting, Trent in his boxers and Tia in her Bryant jersey once more, at the dinette table in her makeshift dining room. He'd mentioned her lack of furniture and she'd simply shrugged, saying "Less is more." The flippant remark had been just on the outskirts of desolate but Trent refused to delve any further. The need to know the reasons behind each word she said, each action she took, was becoming a habit of his that he wasn't sure he liked.

Now, he was completely fascinated by how such a mundane task like eating a slice of pizza could totally arouse him. Especially after their latest round of sex. He should have been completely tapped out, yet here he was sitting across from her watching her chew and savor the pizza as if it were the best she'd ever had, all the while sporting a horrendous hard-on.

"What are you looking at?" she asked after chewing and swallowing. Placing her slice on the paper plate she lifted a napkin and wiped her mouth.

"You," he answered simply.

"Why?" She shrugged. "You've seen me a million times, I'm sure."

"But I've never seen you like this. Relaxed, without makeup, without fancy clothes. It's different."

She'd been about to lift her pizza to her mouth again but she refrained, tilting her head to stare at him. "So do I look that bad?"

"No. On the contrary, you're beautiful." That sounded trite and completely clichéd so he started again. "I'm sure you already know that considering your occupation as a model. You're probably used to people telling you how good you look all the time. But see, the thing is, you're beautiful without all those trappings."

She continued to look at him as if she couldn't believe what he was saying. Hell, he could scarcely believe it.

"You don't fit the whole model persona. Look at you sitting here eating that pizza when you know full well it's going to add pounds to that already fierce body of yours."

That made her smile. "You're right, I'm going to have to work like hell to burn off these calories," she quipped then lifted her slice and took another heaping bite.

Trent couldn't help but laugh. "Contradictions. That's what you are. A bundle of contradictions."

"Is that good or bad?" she asked when her mouth was no longer full.

"I like you better this way," was his reply.

Leaning forward with her elbows on the table she eyed him knowingly. "Point blank, you like me better naked."

Taking a drink of his soda Trent agreed. "Yeah, I definitely like you naked."

As if it were her turn to analyze him she said, "You're different from what I thought, too."

"I am? How?"

"You're the big bad Donovan brother. The mean-ass Navy SEAL that takes no prisoners. Of the Triple Threat you are the most infamous."

Trent didn't bristle at her reference to the name he and his brothers had learned to embrace.

"When Linc married Jade everybody was shocked, yet pleased because college sweethearts *should* have happy endings. Adam and Camille were simply the sweetest fairy tale you could ever see. I see why the press are eating this engagement up as if they were royalty."

"And then there's you." She tilted her head, her braids slipping over her shoulder.

He loved her hair, the color, the style, it fit her perfectly. Sassy and sexy. "I'm just me. There's no mystery there."

She was about to tell him what she really thought of him. As intimate as they had been in the past week, this was as close as they'd come to a normal date. In which case, the first impressions should mean less. Then why was he suddenly on guard about what she was about to say?

"I knew a woman you dated once."

He lifted a brow. There was a long list of women he'd dated and she could possibly know any number of them.

"Her name was Olivia. We had some modeling gigs together a few months back. She couldn't help bragging about her night with the legendary Trent Donovan."

Flipping through his mental Rolodex Trent tried to recall an Olivia who had been a model. Traditionally he wasn't drawn to the model types because they seemed more focused on how they looked than on who they were. Yet here he was with Tia, one of the hottest models on the market. Then again, he admitted, she'd been breaking all sorts of records since the day he'd met her. Especially in the bedroom.

"So what did this Olivia have to say about me?"

"It was pretty much the norm. You're handsome, you're rich and great in bed." Letting the tip of her finger slide across her chin she continued to assess him. "I wonder if I should give her a call just to let her know that her evaluation of you was inaccurate."

"Inaccurate?" Trent asked. "So I'm not good in bed?"

Tia picked up her glass, took a long drink, then sat it back on the table. With a swipe of her tongue over her lips she said, "You're outstanding in bed."

That part of Trent that was all man and all ego couldn't help but be overjoyed. But as he sat back in his chair continuing to stare at the woman across from him, he wondered if that was all she saw in him. Was it just the good-looking, unobtainable Donovan brother who could rock her world in bed? And if so, why did that bother him so much?

"Another thing Olivia didn't mention, and this may be because you only spent that one night with her that I know of. You're extremely dedicated to your family. Your brothers love and respect you, their significant others love you. And your feelings for them are just as fierce. I listen to Camille talking about the relationship between the three of you and I feel almost jealous."

"Really? You don't have any siblings?" he asked although he already knew the answer.

"No. I'm an only child. My mother had a string of miscarriages before she was finally able to carry me to term. After that they didn't dare try again."

"So you were lonely growing up?"

"Not necessarily lonely. I had a lot of friends. Girls I hung out with, kids in the neighborhood. But it's different with siblings. They're always there, from the time you get up in the morning until the time you fall into bed at night.

Most friendships never compare to the closeness of sibling relationships."

Trent nodded. He could completely agree. He'd never had a friend that was closer to him than his brothers were. "So I guess that means you're planning to have a lot of kids. You know, to make sure they have the siblings that you didn't have."

He should have known the question was a mistake. Considering all the information he'd collected on her, he should have steered completely clear of the baby discussion with her. And yet, a part of him desperately wanted to know her plans for the future.

From the instant set of her shoulders as she shifted in the chair, Trent knew he'd made a mistake.

She straightened, brought herself closer to the table, then looked down at her half-eaten slice of pizza. "I don't think much about having kids," she answered quietly.

And as if he just couldn't leave well enough alone, Trent asked, "Why? You'd probably be a great mother."

She looked up at him then, her eyes the saddest orbs he'd ever seen. "Motherhood isn't in the cards for every woman."

Trent got the message loud and clear. She didn't want to talk about this. And once the conversation was started he realized he shouldn't want to talk about it, either. Kids and a family weren't in the cards for him any more than they were for her, but for a whole different set of reasons.

His job was dangerous. He was away for weeks, sometimes months at a time fighting enemies that others only read about in the newspapers. At any time he could be killed. And what would that do to the wife and kids he'd left at home? It was bad enough he had his family that worried about him constantly. No way was he going to put any more people into that situation of worrying over him and possibly the pain of losing him. He just wouldn't do it. So despite the reasons the public had given for him being one of the Triple Threat Donovans, Trent's reason was deeper, more personal than anyone could ever imagine.

"I can't wait until Jade has the twins," he said thinking that was the closest he'd ever get to kids and a family of his own. "Seeing Linc as a father is going to be so weird. My parents are thrilled. You would think they were having another child of their own."

"Jade is going to be great with those babies," Tia said with sincerity. "I'm really happy for her and for Linc."

The fact that she may never again feel that type of happiness cast a melancholy mood over Tia and she lifted her pizza to take another bite.

Trent interrupted her pity party, his smile and blatant sexual desire a pleasant distraction. For that she was grateful. He'd ordered pizza, with extra cheese, her absolute favorite cheat food. She hadn't been lying when she'd said she'd need to work out extrahard to get rid of these calories. But she didn't care. She needed all the comfort she could get.

It suddenly hit her that during this second year anniversary of the worst time in her life, Trent Donovan should be the one getting her through the roughest times. And he didn't even know it.

"So you're truly a Navy SEAL?" she asked hoping to change the subject before her emotions overtook her. "But you're not actively listed in the military, how does that work?"

"I'm listed," he said appearing to be perfectly content on changing the subject. "It's just with a covert group that only goes out on special operations."

"Ooh, like spy-type assignments?" His job sounded so intriguing.

"Something like that. Actually, we act on information from government agents. Our operations usually lead us to threats of national security."

"So, like terrorists or just high-profile criminals?"

"More along the lines of terrorist organizations in the States and abroad."

"Wow."

"Yeah, that's what I used to think myself. Lately, however, I've been dabbling in P.I. work."

"Really? Why the shift?"

Trent shrugged. "I don't know. Maybe because it keeps me local. I know my mother hates when I'm so far away. And my brothers are settling down, having kids. I'd like to see my nieces and nephews growing up."

She nodded. "Look at you, a protector of our country. I'm impressed." He smiled and she thought she'd never seen a more attractive man.

There seemed to be more to Trent, beyond his good looks and obvious sex appeal. Something that she had a feeling people tended to overlook.

"And that's why you won't settle down, isn't it?" she asked suddenly.

The look he gave her said he hadn't expected her to say that but Tia sensed she wasn't completely off the mark.

"My parents worry about me a lot when I'm on a mission. And so do my brothers. It's dangerous enough out there without having to worry about how my safety will affect even more people than that."

"Like a wife and kids?"

"As you said about motherhood, being a husband and a father is simply not in the cards for everyone."

Tia nodded. His comment served to say that he didn't want to talk about this any more than she wanted to talk about children. So for the time that Trent was here they would stay on mutual ground.

"Before we go any further I need to clarify something," she started.

"And what's that?" He pushed away from the table, standing and moving closer to her.

Tia stood, as well. She was tall at five feet ten inches, still Trent towered at least seven inches taller. His stance exuded the strength and protection that Tia subconsciously craved. If only she could fall into his arms, knowing without a doubt that his strength would heal her, his protection would encompass her. But she knew she couldn't. To feel that way again about another man just set her up for the tremendous hurt of loss. She knew that just as surely as everyone lived, they died. And it was the dying that scared her the most.

"This thing between us, whatever it is that we're doing," she stumbled over the words as her mind reeled with more serious thoughts.

He grabbed her hands bringing them up to his lips and kissed each one. "'This thing'?" he questioned.

"I mean, what we're doing…ah, sleeping together…or…" Damn, she couldn't even get it out.

"Lovers, Tia. That's what we are now," he said smoothly pulling her up against his chest.

She nodded. "Okay. Well, since we're lovers. I need you to know that I only do one at a time. I'm not into sharing." There, she'd finally got it out. She only hoped he didn't misread her words to think that she wanted some type of commitment from him.

He simply smiled, wrapping her arms around his neck then grasping her just beneath her buttocks and lifting her until her legs entwined around his waist.

"Then we have something in common. I've never been good at sharing, either."

He was already walking toward the bedroom. Her center throbbed with anticipation, her breasts rubbing wantonly against his chest. "So for the time being, there's nobody else, for either of us, right?"

"Right," he said leaning forward to suckle her lower lip into his mouth. "For the time being," he said releasing her mouth, "Tia St. Claire, you are all mine."

He sat her gently on the bed, pulling her jersey quickly over her head then stepping out of his boxers. Her mouth watered at the sight of his thick arousal stretching upward toward his muscled abs.

Licking her lips as she lay back on the bed, opening herself up to him, Tia whispered, "That's just fine with me."

"Stop whining, we're just going out to get some air," Trent said as he waited impatiently for Tia to slip on her sweatpants and shirt.

"It's almost midnight," she complained.

"I know. That's the best time for a walk."

"No, that's normally the best time to sleep." Pulling her shirt on, she flipped her braids through the collar and stood to stare at him with annoyance.

Taking her hand, Trent pulled her out of the room, heading for the front door. "It's quiet and the humidity has usually gone down so you're not sweating bullets as you walk."

"But my bed felt so good."

"It did," Trent readily agreed. "And you felt beyond good in it." Keeping her hand in his, he made a right turn and led her toward the opening of the apartment complex.

"Obviously not better than the cool night air," she snapped.

For the next few moments they walked in silence until

Trent pulled her in front of him, cradling her back against his front. "Look up," he instructed.

Tia tilted her head back as best she could with his massive chest so close behind her. "What am I looking for?"

"What do you see?"

"It's dark."

Trent chuckled. "Come on, relax and look at the sky. Tell me what you see."

He'd bent his head closer so that the warmth of his breath kissed her cheek. She inhaled then exhaled and gave it a try. "It's like the sea, a deep, dark abyss capable of swallowing secrets, burying fear."

Trent wasn't really surprised that her mind would instantly relate the darkness to fear. Her accident had happened at night, her greatest loss had happened when the sky was a deep, dark abyss.

"I see hope," he told her. "If I stand here and watch long enough, the deep indigo will lighten, gorgeous golds and reds will peek through. The sun will rise and daylight will come, a new day with new events. The hope of tomorrow."

His words were worth so much more than any therapy session Tia had ever participated in. Hope. That's what she should have for her future. Not this innate sense that she was forever doomed to wallow in sadness. With a jolt she pulled out of his arms. Too much, too soon, she thought.

"So how often do you walk at night?" She began moving, walking slowly until he caught her drift and picked up pace beside her.

"Whenever I get the chance. You only work out at the gym?"

"Yes. Carlo is great and can always fit me into his schedule."

"I'll bet he does."

With a tilt of her head she stared at him. "I don't believe it, the infamous Trent Donovan is jealous."

"Whoa. Don't talk so loud, someone might hear you and start a rumor. I am not jealous."

Tia laughed. "It's after midnight. Who's going to be outside to hear us? If anybody is up at this hour they're down on the Strip losing their week's pay. And I know jealous when I see it. Although I don't know why— Carlo's just my trainer. He's not my…" Her words trailed off.

"He's not your lover," Trent finished for her, wondering why it was so hard for her to say that. "And he'd better be real clear on that fact in the future." The mere thought of Carlo or any other man touching her had Trent's temples pounding. Hell, yeah, he was jealous, and that made him even more lethal.

"Carlo's engaged to a really nice blonde who works at one of the bars at MGM Grand."

"Good for him."

He'd pulled her hand into his again as they'd turned at the end of the street two blocks away from the apartment complex, and headed back. They weren't talking a lot at the moment but that was okay. Every now and then Trent would look up to the sky and Tia would follow suit.

She could walk like this for hours with him. It was a bit of a shock to realize that she and Trent Donovan could spend time together without having sex. It was a comforting revelation, one she would no doubt contemplate all day tomorrow.

Tomorrow, she thought wistfully. What would tomorrow bring? Would Trent be in her bed in the morning? Would he want to do something else with her, like have lunch or dinner or simply take another walk at midnight? It had been so long since she'd thought about what tomorrow would bring, so long since the thought had held any appeal for her.

But Trent had given her that. He'd given her tomorrow. He'd given her hope.

Chapter 10

It was almost noon when Tia climbed out of bed on Saturday morning. She and Trent had spent another long night exploring each other's bodies. And just as she had every night, after the first one, she'd sent him home.

Spending one night wrapped in his arms had been a mistake. While she was cool having sex with him, she didn't want to confuse things. They were just lovers, they were not a couple.

So she worked during the day, well, not all day. CK Davis Designs had her pretty much booked through the next couple of months but they didn't have a runway show planned until early spring. So for now work for Tia consisted of three to four hours of photo shoots for newspapers, magazines and the CK Davis catalog. The rest of her time was either spent in the gym or closed in her apartment.

Since Jake and Jessica's deaths she hadn't been out to

dinner or the movies or done much socializing or hanging out at all. She hadn't wanted to do any of those things. She felt guilty for being the sole survivor. And how could life ever be rich and enjoyable again after the unbearable heartache she'd endured? She didn't think it could.

Today, she was moving even slower than usual. Trent had left around three this morning so she'd had more than eight hours of sleep. She shouldn't be moving in this sluggish manner but her destination was playing a big part in her mood.

Jade's baby shower was in two hours.

An elaborate luncheon had been planned to celebrate the arrival of the first Donovan grandchildren. These would be the most famous twins in Las Vegas history for some time. The press were chomping at any tidbits they could gather regarding Jade and the sex of the twins. But Linc was determined to keep the secret. So determined that Trent had even paid Jade's doctor a surprise visit, telling him in no uncertain terms what would happen if the sex of the twins became public.

When he'd told her that Tia had laughed, then she realized he was quite serious. Trent was not a man to be crossed. And he would do whatever was necessary to protect the people he loved.

Stepping into the shower Tia thought seriously about that. What type of woman would capture Trent's heart? In the last two weeks she'd had time to get to know him better than she thought any woman had in a really long time. And over this time she'd confirmed what she already knew— Trent Donovan was a great catch. He was everything a woman could ever dream of in a man. Handsome, protective and fiercely loyal. So why did she continuously put him out of her house?

The answer was easy: Tia wasn't looking for what every other woman was. She'd had it once and it was taken away from her.

No sense putting herself in a position to be hurt again. She didn't think she'd be able to take it.

Turning her back on the spray of water, she let her forehead rest on the tiled wall of the shower.

Yes, Jake and Jessica had been taken from her through a power too high for her to question. But in those first months she'd done just that. Asking God why He'd done something so cruel and so heartless to her had been futile and as her mother had told her, just plain disrespectful. God did not make mistakes, Madeline had said.

And after a while Tia had begun to believe her. Well, she'd actually remembered that she'd believed that all along. Through her pain of losing them she realized that the plan for their life just didn't include her. And she'd started to accept that. Throughout that time she'd also begun to accept something else: that her life obviously did not entail that type of happiness.

As good a catch as Trent was, he wasn't meant to be her catch. They were having fun together but that was as far as it would go. He would not be falling in love with her, nor she with him. That was not their fate.

When she was through showering Tia stood in the mirror taking an extreme amount of time to style her hair. Each time Trent saw her and she'd had it up he'd simply taken it down. While they had sex he would continuously thread his fingers through the tiny braids. He liked when they draped over onto his chest as she rode him, or fanned out on the pillow as he moved on top of her. And when she realized that the reason she was fussing with her hair so fervently was because she wanted to do something that he would like, she immediately stopped. Leaving the top pulled up with a clear clip and the rest hanging down her back.

Going to her closet, she decided on dark, flare-leg jeans and a yellow blouse. Her yellow Donna Karan jeweled sandals were one of her favorites and she sat on the bed to tie the thin straps around her ankles. Standing before the wall-length mirror, she surveyed herself and liked what she saw.

The ride to the Donovan estate would take her about forty minutes. Checking her clock she realized she'd taken a little too long on her hair and had exactly forty minutes to get to the shower on time. She hated being late for anything. Moving into the living room she spotted the box that had been delivered yesterday afternoon. For the shower gift, she'd decided on a double changing table with a cascade trim and honey-oak finish. Camille had mentioned that Jade was designing the nursery with oak furniture and shades of yellow and green. The changing table was beautiful and would fit into the décor splendidly.

Grabbing her purse and her keys, Tia lifted the box and headed out the door. She was allotted two parking spots for her apartment and always parked in the one closest to the mailboxes. Getting closer to her car she noticed that she had a flat tire. She was in the process of cursing when she came around to the other side of the car and noticed that tire, too, was flat. Propping the box up against the door she went to the back intending to open the trunk and get out her spare when she noticed that the back two tires were flat, as well.

"Dammit!" she swore.

There was no way she could wait for the auto club to come and fix the tires and get to the baby shower at a respectable time. And as much as she didn't really want to go she didn't want to disappoint Camille, either. With that thought in mind she reached into her purse and pulled out her cell phone.

"Hello?" Camille answered sounding a little winded.

"Hi, Camille. It's me, Tia."

"Hey, Tia. What's up? Are you on your way?"

"I was but I have a flat. Or rather a couple of flat tires. If you're not too busy do you think you could pick me up?"

"You know I would but I'm already at the house trying to get some last minute things together. But wait, Adam just walked in. I'll see if he can pick you up. Hold on."

"No, that's…" Tia was about to tell her that was okay but in the background she could hear Camille asking her fiancé to come and pick her up.

"Okay, it's all set. Adam said he'll be there within the hour," Camille said returning to the phone.

"That's okay, Camille, I just won't come. I don't want to inconvenience anyone."

"It's not an inconvenience. Adam left our gift at the house so he's heading out toward your direction anyway. Just sit tight, he'll be there soon."

Closing the phone Tia decided not to go back into her apartment. If she did she knew she'd come up with another reason not to go to the shower. So instead she walked around the car noticing that not only were the tires flat, they'd been slashed so that the rubber was hanging out in jagged intervals.

Looking around she tried to see if this was a group act of vandalism or just her car. None of the other vehicles in the lot were affected. Taking a deep breath she opened the door to her car and took a seat, turning on the radio to listen and wait for her ride.

* * *

Trent was more than an hour late for the shower. It wasn't a big deal since this get-together was more for the women of the family. Still, Jade had insisted that Linc be there. And in turn Linc had browbeaten his brothers into enduring the torture with him.

Pulling up behind a line of cars coming out of his parents' driveway, Trent got out and walked toward the house. He wasn't at all surprised to see his brothers along with his cousins Max, Ben and Brandon standing out front, beers in hand.

"What's going on? You guys get kicked out of the party?" he joked.

"You try sitting in a room full of women talking about the joys and pains of pregnancy," Max joked extending his hand for Trent to shake.

"Yeah, every few minutes they'd realize men were in the room and then we'd get these sizzling looks as if all the pain and dreariness of pregnancy were our fault." This was Brandon Donovan whom Trent was completely surprised to see. Brandon lived in Houston, where, last Trent heard, he was a junior investor working for a new but solvent hedge fund called TJB Investments.

Brandon was Uncle Albert's son whose mother had passed away seven years ago. Since then Uncle Albert hadn't been to many of the family gatherings. Brandon and Bailey, his twin sister, tended to stick close to their father, keeping an eye on him. Their adopted brother Brock lived in Maryland and didn't come to many family functions.

"Well, well, well. What brings you out to Sin City, little cousin?" Trent asked thumping fists with Brandon then giving him a hug.

"It's not everyday one of the Triple Threats prepares to be a father," Brandon said, smiling at Linc.

"True. Congratulations again, man." Trent shook Linc's hand, then caught the questioning glare Adam was giving him.

"What's up, Adam?"

"I'm just wondering where your head is at right now."

"Not now, Adam," Linc warned.

Trent was confused. The last time he'd seen his brothers they'd left things on an even keel. "What's the problem?"

"I had to pick your woman up today. Where were you?" Adam said, ignoring Linc's glare.

"Whoa, what are you talking about 'my woman'?"

"Yeah, you know Trent doesn't keep one woman," Ben joked.

"Look at him, he doesn't even know which one you're talking about," Max added.

Trent, however, wasn't getting the joke. "Speak your mind, Adam, and stop beating around the bush."

"Okay. Tia's car was vandalized. She called Camille for a ride so I went to pick her up."

"What? When was this? I didn't know anything about something happening to her car."

"Oh, I forgot. You're only interested in sleeping with her, not making sure she's safe."

Where was this coming from? And why was Adam giving him this attitude? Trent knew the answer—he'd known that getting involved with Tia was going to be too personal for Adam because of Camille.

"Trent has a right to lead his own life, Adam. We can't change the man he is," Linc said.

"But is he a man? I mean, really? When are you going to grow up and start taking…"

Trent was in his face in seconds; the other Donovan men stepping either behind Adam or behind him, ready to pull the two of them apart. "First off, you're still wet behind your ears with your nose wide open for Camille. I don't say anything about that because it's your business. Just like what goes on between Tia and me is my business."

Adam, while not a SEAL, *was* a Donovan, he didn't back down. "The world doesn't revolve solely around you, Trent. If you don't want her then leave her alone. But don't treat her like you treat the rest of your flings. If she gets hurt, Camille will not only want to castrate you, I'll have to hear it every night for the rest of my life."

"Tia's a grown woman, Adam. I doubt she needs you or Camille worrying about her." Trent didn't have time for this. The last thing he wanted was to interrupt Linc's day. Apparently his presence was doing just that. He turned to walk away but remembered something Adam said.

"What did you mean by 'keeping her safe'? Was she there when her car was vandalized?"

"She had to have been. When I got there she said she hadn't left the apartment since last night when she was with you," Adam said in a clipped voice.

Trent's mind whirled. After their walk they'd returned to her apartment, where she'd insisted he needed to go home. While a huge part of him wanted to stay, Trent wasn't ready to acknowledge that urging and waited until she'd fallen asleep before leaving. He hadn't checked her car before he pulled off, hadn't thought there was a need to.

"What are you thinking?" Max asked, giving Trent a knowing look.

"Nothing," Trent answered quickly.

Ben took another sip of his beer. "It was probably just some kids fooling around."

"Yeah," Trent said absently. "Probably just some kids."

But the sudden alertness of his body and the tingling at the base of his neck said differently.

Tia had been enjoying herself for the half hour she'd been at the shower. During the ride with Adam she'd had thoughts of telling him to turn around and take her back home. But that was childish. She could do this. She would do this.

Arriving at the house of Linc and Jade Donovan, she'd been amazed by the beautiful grounds and expert décor throughout the house. The shower was mainly situated in the dining room, leading out to the wraparound deck. Streamers, balloons and yellow and green baby parapher-nalia decorated the room throughout. Long tables covered in white linen cloths with tiny embroidered teddy bars along the edge held so much food that Tia thought she'd be sick. There was everything from deviled eggs to salmon and caviar. It was clear that no expense would be spared for these babies.

"So what'd you get her?" Noelle, Jade's younger sister, asked as she took the seat next to Tia.

She'd come out onto the deck trying to get a moment of quiet. There were so many women in the house that she'd smiled and talked as much as if she were at a press conference.

But Noelle was extremely nice and very down to earth. Having been new to the Donovan family at one time she was trying to find her place, as well. So Tia felt they at least had that in common.

"Dual changing tables," she answered.

"Huh, why didn't I think of that?"

Tia grinned. "What did you get her?"

"I didn't have a clue. What do you buy the woman who

has everything? Fantastic, rich husband who loves her to distraction. Gorgeous house. Successful business. And now she's pregnant with twins and still as beautiful as ever." Noelle sighed. "Can you tell I hate her?"

"No. But I can tell you really love your sister. You've been running around here making sure that everything is where it should be as well as making sure Jade's comfortable. As much as you and Linc fuss over her I'm surprised she's even allowed to walk by herself."

Noelle laughed. "I know, complete overkill. But she's my sister and she's looked out for me for so long. I'm happy for her."

Tia looked at Noelle with her burnt orange complexion and laughing gray eyes. She was a striking beauty with shoulder length hair and a gorgeous smile. When she'd first met her Tia wondered why she didn't model. But then Camille had informed her that Noelle had just received her business degree and was working for Linc at the Gramercy Casino. Brains and beauty, she was a killer package that some smart man was quickly going to scoop up.

"She and Linc are going to be great parents," Tia said wistfully.

"Yeah."

They sat in silence for all of two minutes before Noelle said what was really on her mind.

"So what's up with you and Trent? I hear you've been kickin' it lately."

How had she heard that? Tia didn't even have to ask. The Donovan brothers were extremely close. Trent probably told them and Adam told Camille. As an only child Tia never had to deal with her business being spread about the family.

"We're just friends," she answered and felt a thud in her chest at the proclamation.

Noelle apparently didn't believe those words because she turned to stare at Tia with an "and I'm Queen Elizabeth" look.

"Trent does not have women 'friends,'" she quipped.

"Oh really? Well, what does he have?"

"Lovers," Noelle said without hesitation.

And that's exactly what they were. "So why ask if you already knew?"

Noelle shrugged not remotely embarrassed by her prodding. "The female version of simply sexual relationships is always better than the male."

They both laughed at that. "You've got that right," Tia said. She liked Noelle Vincent. The woman was smart and fun and picked up on everything. She suspected that's why Linc had been singing her praises at the casino.

"Come on, they're about to open the gifts," Noelle said, standing from her seat. "You don't want to miss all the Gucci booties and Versace sleepers."

Tia stood with her. "No, we definitely don't want to miss that."

Twenty minutes later Tia was sitting on the couch, matriarch Beverly Donovan on one side and Noelle on the other. Jade had begun opening the mountain of presents that had been bought for either her or the twins.

As Tia watched her open a box with a white velour Donna Karan robe she wondered why she hadn't just brought Jade a present for herself, instead of putting herself through the trauma of picking out a baby gift.

"That was beautiful," Beverly Donovan whispered to Tia.

Tia nodded. She and Beverly had spoken briefly on the

occasions they'd met at Camille's parties or showings. But today, Tia noted the woman made an attempt to talk to her a little more. She wondered if it was because of the open knowledge that she and Trent were sleeping together.

Jade was now opening the box with the double stroller. Next followed a box full of sleepers and undershirts. Tia figured the room was filled with at least fifty women. More of the Donovan family, some of Jade's employees, Camille and Noelle. Yet Tia felt as if the crowd were bigger. The room suddenly seemed smaller, tight.

From somewhere in the room a camera flashed. Women clapped and cooed, loving each gift that Jade opened. Tia's vision blurred a bit as she felt her cheeks lifting in what she hoped was a smile. Jade was opening another box, it appeared heavy, too heavy for her to lift. Camille, who had been standing beside her, helped, pushing the box across the floor in front of Jade instead of picking it up. Jade leaned forward, her protruding stomach resting between her legs. With perfectly manicured nails she began tearing at the cheerfully wrapped box.

Tia felt as if a lead weight had been dropped on her chest. She closed her eyes for a brief moment, tried to inhale slowly, to ease the pain away. It didn't work.

When she opened her eyes Jade was smiling, Linc had brought her a rocking chair that looked to be antique. She'd had a rocking chair similar to that in Jessica's nursery. Sounds thundered in her head.

In a flash she was back in the car, buckled in the passenger seat. They were returning from a party where Jake had wanted her to meet with some folks at *Vogue* regarding another cover spot and pictures of the baby when she gave birth. They were in a great mood as the *Vogue* execs were ecstatic that she had agreed.

Tia thought about the many to-do items on her wedding-planning list. A couple of months after the baby's birth she and Jake were going to be married. All was well in their lives. Then she saw the headlights. They seemed huge, their glare bursting through the front windshield like an explosion. She heard horns, glass crashing, felt the jolt of impact, Jake yelling, her screaming.

In the next moment a pain Tia had never felt before traveled over her stomach. She buckled over. Breathing had become laborious as she struggled to stand. She felt hands on her arm. Heard someone calling her name. But her focus was on getting up, getting out of here.

Her legs shook and she stumbled out of the room. There was someone behind her, a female. She was yelling for water or ice or something. Tia couldn't really tell. All she knew was that there was a door somewhere, a door that would lead her outside and outside would lead her home, where she was safe.

Finding it she wrenched it open. Her chest burned with every bit of air she inhaled. Her stomach hurt and threatened to retrieve everything she'd eaten today. Cool air tapped at her face but did nothing to ease this turmoil. Looking up she thought she saw the sun then the sky instantly went black, just like that night. The night they'd crashed.

"Tia! Tia! Are you okay?"

She heard the female voice again but needed to get away from it. It was just the nurses. The doctor had told her that Jake was dead. Jessica was dead. The nurses tried to help, to comfort her, but it was no use.

Running, or at least she thought she was running. Her feet were moving, everything around her seemed to be in motion. Tears stung her eyes, she had no clue where she was going, only that she desperately needed to get away.

Abruptly all her movement was stopped. She'd run into a wall? She was falling, no she was floating. Had she died, as well? Oh God, please say it was finally over. Please say He decided to take her instead of Jake and Jessica. Please, please.

Chapter 11

He'd heard screaming and his military instincts had immediately kicked in.

From the group in which he'd stood and been talking, Trent turned. What he saw frightened him more than any battle he'd ever been in.

Tia was stumbling out the front door of the house. She'd taken one step and her legs had almost given out. She looked like she was about to faint. Right behind her was his mother, Noelle and Camille. They were all calling her name and reaching for her. But she pulled away, stumbling down the next step. How she managed to stand through the tears streaming down her face and the ruthless shaking of her head Trent had no idea. But in the next instant he was running to her, scooping her up into his arms the minute he was close enough.

Her breaths came in ragged spurts. She mumbled incoherently, tears springing from her eyes as if someone had released a dam.

"Call an ambulance," his mother was saying behind him.

"She was fine a moment ago," Camille was at his side as he walked with Tia in his arms.

"Go back inside," he told her tightly.

"No!" Camille yelled. "Where are you taking her? You should wait for the paramedics. Something's wrong, Trent!"

"She's going to be fine, Camille," Trent heard Adam trying to console his fiancé.

"Slow down, man. Where are you taking her?" Adam asked.

"She's going with me! I'll take care of her," Trent said, finally stopping when he was at the passenger side of his truck. He tried to reach into his pocket for his keys but Tia was still thrashing in his arms. He had to get her away from here, to calm her down and find out what had happened.

His heart pounded, tiny sharp jabs spearing his chest each time she whimpered, at each tear he watched stream from her eyes.

He felt a heavy hand on his back, then going into his jacket pocket. Turning slightly he saw that it was Linc. He was getting his keys and unlocking the door.

"Call if you need anything," Linc told him when the door was open and he was slipping Tia onto the seat.

Pulling back Trent closed the door, stood and could only stare at Linc for what seemed like an endless second. In his brother's eyes he saw trust.

Linc trusted that he would take care of Tia. He didn't believe he was going to hurt her, a change from his reaction a couple of weeks ago. Trent couldn't speak, but nodded and ran around to the driver's side and jumped in.

He drove like a madman he knew, but the farther away

from the house he traveled, the calmer Tia seemed to get. With one hand on the steering wheel and the other touching her anywhere he could, rubbing her arms, wiping what tears he could away from her face, trying to hold her hand, he drove as best he could.

His house was closer so he turned off the interstate and headed towards his condo without another thought. Her chest heaved and she hugged her stomach as if the pain was unbearable. In less than fifteen minutes Trent was pulling into his complex, shaving twenty minutes off the usual driving distance between his and Linc's homes.

He was out of the car with Tia in his hands in minutes, walking as fast as he could toward the building's front doors. Once inside, he saw Lyle, the concierge, lifting a brow in his direction. Trent sent him a scathing glare and Lyle immediately came from behind the desk.

"What can I do for you, Mr. Donovan? Shall I call a doctor?" The tall thin man was walking beside Trent looking up at him, then down at Tia.

"Order some food, I don't care what, and have it sent up immediately," Trent said watching as Lyle jabbed the button to summon the elevator.

Stepping inside Trent pulled Tia closer to his chest. She was moaning now, a pitiful sound that ripped at his self-control. What had happened to her in that house?

Once in his apartment Trent moved instantly to his bedroom, laying Tia down gently. He stood, was going to go into the bathroom to wet a towel for her and wipe her face but she reached up to him, her fingers clutching as if she were trying to grab at something.

"Please. Please. Take me…instead," she whimpered. Then her head thrashed back and forth on the pillow. "No. No. Everybody leaves. Please, don't leave."

Trent was confused and then again he wasn't. Sitting on the bed he gathered her up in his arms, pulling her onto his lap and cradled her.

Rubbing his hands over her hand, across her cheek, he rocked her, whispering as he did.

"It's okay, baby. It's all over. It was just an accident, Tia. It's all over now."

After a few minutes her thrashing stopped, her heart still pounded, he felt it with each tremble of her body. She was still crying, silently now, not those gut wrenching sobs that were tearing at his control.

"It's all right, baby. You go ahead and cry. Everything's going to be all right." He was telling her wondering how he was going to make that a reality.

For once in his life Trent felt completely helpless. A semiautomatic weapon and a good strategy wasn't going to win this battle.

What ailed Tia wasn't an enemy he could hunt down and kill to protect her. It was an inner demon that would haunt her as long as she allowed it. And Trent, no matter how much he wanted to, didn't know how to exorcise that.

He had no experience in this area, never having dealt with women on an emotional level. Adam thought he didn't give a damn about Tia, thought he was going to use her and dismiss her as he had the other women in his life—and for a while he'd thought to do the same. Yet here she was, in his arms, clinging to him as if her life depended on it.

"They're gone," she said her voice sounding tiny in the big space of his room.

He nodded his head. "I know, baby."

"They died and they're not coming back."

"It's all right. They're in a better place now."

She shifted, then pulled away from him slightly.

"Trent?" she asked as if for the first time realizing it was he who held her.

"Hi," he said weakly, lifting a hand to smooth her hair back from her face.

She reached up with shaking hands trying to wipe the tears from her face. He pushed her hands away and used his fingers to do the job himself.

"How did I get here? Where am I?" she was asking looking around the room.

"Calm down. I brought you to my house because it was closer than trying to take you to yours."

"What happ—" she was about to say then her eyes flew to his again. "You said you know. What do you know?"

Trent knew she was going to be pissed off but he didn't care. Tia needed to talk to someone. From what Adam had told him, Camille didn't know about the accident so she couldn't help.

Originally Trent had no intention of confessing to Tia about his look into her past but that was because he hadn't wanted to deal with her on this level. Now, things had changed.

"I know about Jake and Jessica and the car accident that killed them."

She tried to squirm off his lap but Trent held her still. "It's okay, baby. It's okay to cry and to scream. You lost the people you loved most in this world. It's okay to be upset."

"How did you know? How did you find out?"

"The information was there, Tia. All I had to do was look."

"You looked into my past?"

"Yes."

"Why?"

That one question had him stumped. Despite what his brothers thought, Trent did not go through the time and trouble to investigate every woman that he slept with. But from the start he'd known that Tia wasn't like every other woman. He'd seen something in her eyes, heard something in her voice that said she was dealing with a situation that she couldn't handle on her own. It was instinctive that he try to help, it was his job. He went off to foreign countries trying to save the lives of Americans and other people that he didn't even know. He knew Tia, intimately, why shouldn't he do what he could to save her?

"I knew there was something going on with you and I wanted to help," he said finally, admitting to himself that the need to help her was much stronger than the need to possess her body.

"You had no right," she said looking away from him. "It was my business."

Reaching around he touched her chin, turning her face to his. "And now you are my business."

She leaned forward, letting her head fall into her hands. "It's been two years. You'd think I'd be over these panic attacks by now."

"Have you seen a doctor about them?"

She shook her head even though he'd already known the answer to that.

"Maybe you should."

"No. They'll want me to talk about it, to relive it and I...I just...can't."

Her body trembled and he knew she was crying again. He didn't pull her back into his arms although the need to hold on to her until she was better was powerful. Instead he moved until he was right beside her, simply wrapping an arm around her.

"You have to try to make peace with what happened, Tia. Or you'll never be free to move on with your life."

"I have no life without them!" she screamed and jumped up off the bed.

She was pacing the room back and forth and, for a few minutes, Trent simply let her be. She needed space to regain her footing. He knew Tia was a fiercely independent woman. Leaning on him of all people wasn't going to be easy for her. But in the end, she would. She would trust him to take care of her and to help her through this. Trent would have it no other way.

"Tell me about Jake," he said slowly, still sitting on the bed.

Her pacing slowed. She folded her arms over her chest but continued to walk. "He was my manager. I met him at an audition in New York. We clicked immediately."

"Love at first sight," Trent said tightly, not liking the thought of Tia giving such a deep emotion to another man.

"No," she said stopping suddenly. "We were friends. Really good friends. I used to think of him as a brother at first. Then one night we ended up in bed together." She looked contemplative, then gave a stilted laugh. "I don't even remember how it was that we ended up in bed together. I just know the next morning we woke up naked and smiling."

Okay, she could stop with the trip down memory lane. Trent's jaw was clenching so tight he feared he'd dislodged a few teeth.

"And just like that we were a couple. I got pregnant about six months later and Jake asked me to marry him. Everything happened really fast but it felt right."

"You wanted to marry him and to have his baby?"

"I wanted a family."

Trent nodded, not sure she understood the depth of what she'd just said, or what she didn't say.

"I found out immediately that I was carrying a girl and

we decided on the name Jessica. I had everything all ready for her. The room, her clothes, everything was all planned." She stopped walking. "And then they were gone."

Trent stood then, but didn't go to her. "But you survived. You're still here. Do you think Jake would want you living this shell of a life because you can't let go of your grief?"

"I'm living the best life I can."

"Bull! You're hiding in that apartment, coming out only to work. You're not living at all."

Lifting her head defiantly she retorted, "You don't seem to be complaining when my non-living consists of sleeping with you."

He did walk to her then. "Sex is easy, Tia. It's physical, not emotional," he told her hearing the truth in his words and feeling the pity that he himself believed them so stoically.

She stared up at him, letting his hands go around her waist, her hands hesitantly falling to his chest. "You're wrong. Nothing is easy with you, Trent."

Recognizing that she was probably right, Trent sighed. "It doesn't have to be hard, Tia."

"How else would it be with you? The last of the Triple Threat Donovans with his navy SEAL secret assignments and irrefutable reputation—everything in your life is hard."

Her statement held him quiet.

"I'm sorry you went through this horrible time, but I want to do whatever it takes to make you whole. Do you understand that, Tia? Whatever it takes to keep this from haunting you, I'll do."

Her chest constricted, tears once more stinging her eyes. This was unexpected. He was unexpected.

"I don't want you to do anything."

"I don't need your permission."

"You're a bully," she spat.

"No. I'm just a man who wants what's best for...his woman."

She should have pulled away again. She should have run out of that apartment and back to her own. She was too exposed, too vulnerable. And Trent Donovan was too good, too smooth and too potent for her to ignore. His words wrapped her in a protective cocoon that she'd longed to feel. His hands and his gaze held her perfectly still, and when his head descended, his kiss took her to a place she'd never known. A place she never wanted to leave.

The next clear thought Tia had was around eight o'clock the next morning. That's when she attempted to roll over in bed and found herself face-to-face with Trent.

He was wide awake and looked as if he had been for some time since he was fully dressed, except for shoes. Glancing down quickly at herself she realized she was still fully dressed, as well.

"We just slept, Tia. I'm not into having sex with emotionally distraught women," he said by way of a good morning.

"I wasn't emotionally distraught," she snapped, then attempted to roll in the other direction.

He stopped her by rolling on top of her, pinning her to the mattress. "Don't for one minute believe I didn't want to make love to you all night long. I just like to know that when I'm with a woman, she's with me one hundred percent."

"Point taken," she said, noting his raging erection pressing into her center as he parted her legs.

"As for the emotionally distraught part, don't get all uptight over it. I'm just telling you what you need to hear. What I suspect other people close to you have wanted to say but have not, for fear of hurting your feelings."

"And let me guess, you don't give a damn about my feelings so you'll say what you want."

She tried to break free of his hold but his fingers clamped tightly over her wrists.

"I don't mince words, you know that's not the type of person I am. As for your feelings," he sighed. "I care about your feelings much more than I anticipated I would."

Tia blinked, not sure how she was supposed to react. What she was sure about was that she'd completely embarrassed herself yesterday. She needed to call Camille and apologize to her and the rest of the women of the Donovan clan. But first, she needed to get Trent off her before she made a further fool of herself by begging him to make love to her.

"I need to get home," she said turning her head away from him.

He kept her wrists pulled together then gently held her by the chin. "Yesterday you had a panic attack," he said matter-of-factly.

Tia waved his words away. "I've had them before. I have medication that I refuse to take, given to me by a therapist that I no longer see. It's not a big deal."

He ignored her flippant tone. "Last night you were emotionally distraught over an accident you could neither have prevented nor foreseen. I want you to talk to someone about it. You need to move past this grief or it's going to consume you, Tia.

"And I'm not saying this because I'm the infamous Trenton Donovan, the brother with no feelings and no cares in the world." He paused looking at her earnestly. "I'm saying this because I want you to be well. I want you to be able to go to a baby shower without falling apart, to leave your apartment and socialize without creating barriers to keep everyone at a distance. I want you to live. *You've* got to want to live."

The pain she'd felt in her chest yesterday was nothing compared to the immediate warmth moving through her at this moment. It consumed her, slowly building, then wrapping her heart in a tight little bundle. Why had his words meant so much to her? Why him? Why now?

Too many questions and not enough time to analyze them, she thought. Yet ignoring Trent was never an option.

"Thank you," she said quietly. "Nobody's ever put it quite like that before."

"They should have. But since I'm the one who had to tell you I'll be the one to follow up on your progress." He smiled.

"I didn't say I was going to see anyone," she said, knowing full well it wasn't the response he wanted to hear.

"You should know I'm not a very good negotiator."

"You don't control me, Trent. We're not a couple, we're just lovers, remember." She said the last part with more vehemence than she thought or intended. She didn't want Trent to be anything other than her lover. Right?

She probably should have thought to say that sooner because he jumped off her as if she were the carrier of some deadly disease. Standing a good distance from the bed he said, "Camille used to see this really good therapist. Either I'll get the name and number for you or you can get it yourself. But I'm warning you not to take too long. I don't have a lot of patience." That slow, sweet smile again.

"You don't have a lot of sense," she said moving off the bed and looking for her shoes. "I'm a grown woman. I'm capable of taking care of myself."

She'd just found her other shoe and was standing up when he grabbed her by the shoulders. His front was pressed into her back and he spoke in a soft, but gruff voice directly into her ear.

"This is not a game, Tia. It's your life you're playing with. Now if you don't want me bossing you around then stop being a nitwit and do what we both know is right."

"Let go of me. You have no right," she said icily.

"Now see, that's where you're wrong. Since we are 'lovers' I have every right to touch you when and where I want to. Unless you want to change that, too."

Her entire body went still with his words. What was he asking her now? Tia couldn't think straight. She'd known it wasn't going to be easy dealing with Trent, but this was going over the top. He shouldn't give a damn about her mental health or her feelings for that matter. That's not what they agreed to. It's not what she could handle.

"Do you still want to be my lover, Tia?"

Why was he doing this? Why was he acting so differently from how he was supposed to? He was one of the Triple Threats, he didn't want any serious entanglements. He didn't hold women and tell them that he'd take care of everything for them. That wasn't who he was supposed to be.

"Just let me go, Trent. I need to go to the bathroom and I want to go home."

She hadn't answered his question, yet he'd still let her go. Closing herself in the bathroom she gave a heavy sigh. What the hell was she doing? She couldn't be, shouldn't be…falling in love with Trent Donovan.

"Dammit!" In the living room where Trent had stomped to after she'd closed herself in the bathroom, he slammed his flattened palms down on the bar.

She was right. He wasn't supposed to give a damn if she got help or not. He should never have brought her here. He should have taken her to the hospital or to her house yesterday. And he should have left her alone.

Holding her, rocking her as she cried and dreamed throughout the night had been foolish.

But Trent wasn't one for regrets. It had happened and now he had to make the best of it. The fact was he was worried about her. Had been since that night at Camille's party and that probably wasn't going to stop because they both were now questioning his actions.

Speaking of Camille, he knew she had to be worried sick about what had happened. Neither she nor Adam had looked pleased at him carrying Tia off once more so he decided to give their minds some relief. Reaching for his cell phone he dialed their house number. It was early Sunday morning, they probably weren't even up yet.

"Hello?" Camille answered on the first ring.

So much for sleeping late, Trent thought. "Mornin'," he said clearing his throat.

"Trent? Where's Tia? I tried calling her house? How is she?"

"Whoa. One question at a time, little sis. She's right here with me at my place. And before you get all feisty, I didn't touch her. Well, not in that way." And the thought hadn't crossed his mind. To be quite honest Trent had been more than a little nervous watching Tia's breakdown last night.

Through the phone he could hear Camille releasing a deep breath. "Thank God, I was so worried."

"I know, that's why I called."

"So what happened? I mean, one minute we were all having such a good time and the next she just went off."

"Yeah, well, she's going to have to be the one to tell you about that. I just wanted you to know she's a lot better this morning," he said, looking towards his bedroom expecting her to emerge at any minute.

"I'm going to stop and get her some breakfast and then take her home. She'll probably call you later today." And if she didn't, because he'd gotten the upper hand by calling Camille first, he was sure his soon-to-be sister-in-law would be calling Tia, if not showing up on her doorstep.

"You know what's going on with her, don't you?" Camille asked suddenly.

Trent thought about lying, then figured there was no point. The key was to get Tia the help she needed to deal with her grief. He planned to stay on Tia's back about it but it would help if she had a softer influence like Camille in her corner, as well.

"I do but I'm going to let Tia tell you herself. Besides, she might open up to you a little more than she did to me. I've already overstepped the trust boundaries with her, I'd rather not do it again." For the first time in his life Trent had second thoughts about investigating someone without their knowledge. While he knew that knowing Tia's problems had given him the ability to deal with her breakdown last night, he was sure she didn't like the way he'd found out. And as he'd sat on the bed under her shaky scrutiny he'd felt like crap for disappointing her.

He heard her moving in the other room and decided the ride home with her would go a lot smoother if she didn't catch him on the phone with Camille talking about her. "Listen, tell Adam I'll give him a ring later. I've got to go."

"Okay," Camille said. "And Trent?"

"Yeah?"

"Thanks. You did a really good thing and I'm proud of you."

Why those words had Trent smiling he couldn't quite

say. Except that having Camille and Adam think he was
some kind of deadbeat whose only purpose on this earth
was as a womanizer hadn't been sitting well with him
lately. Knowing that he had some qualities that redeemed
him with them felt good.

"I'm not all bad, Camille."

"I know. It's just taken you so long to realize that."

Trent was just closing his phone when Tia emerged
from the bedroom. She looked tired as hell and still a little
agitated with him. Finding he didn't like either of those
issues, he decided to deal with the latter first.

He moved until he stood directly in front of her. She
looked up at him warily. He didn't touch her but folded his
arms over his chest.

"I apologize for looking into your past. It was wrong. I
should have just asked you what I wanted to know."

She blinked and a look of complete shock covered her
face. "Ah…okay," she said slowly, then shook her head as
if to clear it. "I just didn't think what we were doing
required full disclosure."

Having sex with a woman didn't usually, he agreed with
that. Except for the fact that she was healthy, which he also
covered by using protection, Trent hadn't ever needed to
know much more about the women he slept with. Until Tia.

"It's a habit that comes with the job," he replied.

"Was I a security threat?" she asked with a raise of one
elegantly arched brow.

Only to my sanity, he thought but wisely didn't speak.
"Like I said, it's a habit and I'm sorry."

Tia took another deep breath. "It's okay. I'm kind of glad
you know. And what you said in there," she nodded back
toward the bedroom, "You were right. I do need to try to
move past this grief. I'm so tired of carrying this burden."

She was shaking her head again and Trent ditched the idea of keeping his hands to himself. Instead he wrapped them around her, pulling her tight into his embrace. "Listen, I deal with death all the time. I've lost some team members as well as some good friends in the line of battle. But the one thing I know is that they lived their purpose and I have to live mine. Nowhere is it written that I must carry the guilt of their deaths with me as a reminder."

Dropping her head to rest on his chest she whispered, "I can't just forget them."

"And I'm not asking you to. But you need to forgive yourself for surviving that accident. You need to accept that you are still living and move on."

She chuckled and looked up at him. "You sound like my mother."

"Then your mother must be one smart lady."

"I'm hungry," she said.

"I figured as much. Let's get you fed and back in your apartment." He was leading her to the door when she stopped and wrapped her arms around his neck, pulling his face closer to hers.

When her lips touched his warning bells exploded in Trent's mind. He'd kissed her many times in the last couple of weeks and had enjoyed it immensely. But this kiss was different.

The touch of her lips seemed softer, the swipe of her tongue over his intense but meaningfully so. She guided his mouth in a sensual ride that took Trent's breath away. Was she apologizing? Were they making up? Was he completely losing his mind?

The feeling was foreign to Trent but he could swear this kiss was a declaration of sorts. Her feelings or his, he couldn't quite tell. All he knew for sure, as he once again wrapped her lithe body in his arms and settled in to take the kiss deeper, was that at this moment this was exactly where he wanted to be and whom he wanted to be with.

Somewhere in the back of his mind he knew that the last of the Triple Threats was in deep trouble.

Chapter 12

Before going into Tia's building he asked her to show him her car. She had a nice gunmetal-gray Honda Accord coupe. A couple of weeks ago he would have expected her to have something expensive, more flashy. Now, as he stepped off the curb, crouched down and touched a hand to the ripped rubber of her front tire, he realized this car suited her true understated glamour.

"What time did you finally get up yesterday morning to go to the shower?" he asked remembering he'd left her place a little after three in the morning. Heading to the parking lot at that time of morning he hadn't seen anything suspicious. Then again his body had been sated, his mind still full of the sensuous woman he'd had the pleasure of making love to for more than five hours. But Trent was a soldier, if something were out of place yesterday morning when he'd come out, he would have seen it.

"A little after noon," she said from where she was standing on the sidewalk.

Looking over his shoulder he couldn't help but grin with pride. "Did I tire you out?"

"It figures I'd be attracted to a night owl," she said, looking away as color blotched her cheeks.

The fact that he could make her blush only served to endear her more to Trent. A point he was going to have to find the time to think through. If the feelings he feared he was beginning to develop for Tia St. Claire were going to be a problem for her, he preferred to know sooner rather than later. That was the only way a suitable plan of action could be considered.

"So when you came out at…"

"A little after one," she finished for him. "It takes me forty-five minutes to get to the other side of the city where Jade and Linc live. The shower started at two so I figured I'd arrive right on time."

"And when you came out you saw that all four tires were flat." He was walking around the car now, noticing that each tire was slashed. The cuts jagged, as if done with an angry blade.

"Well, I was carrying the gift. It was a big box so I put it down when I got to the driver's side. That's when I noticed the first flat. I unlocked the doors and was about to open the back door to put the box on the backseat when I saw the other flat. Then I walked around the car and saw the others."

He had just been kneeling, looking under the car. As he suspected there were big wet spots on the ground. Most likely a combination of oil and brake fluid. He stood frowning.

"That's when you called Adam to come and pick you up?"

"No." She shook her head. "I called Camille to see if she

could pick me up on her way. But she was already at the shower. Adam needed to come back to their house to get their gift so she asked him to get me."

She stood there, with her purse dangling from one arm, one hand twirling a braid as if that were the most natural pose in the world. Which was conceivable considering her line of work. The fact that she looked like she was posing for *Playboy* magazine with her skintight jeans and white ribbed tank top that barely held her full breasts in check was just a coincidence. Those heels had to be at least three and a half to four inches high, yet she stood in them like she was wearing house slippers. She was sexy before ten in the morning and wearing clothes she'd had on the day before. His body tightened with desire.

"Why didn't you call me?" he asked moving closer to her. He felt like a predator approaching his prey. His heart thumped methodically as if timing its beat with his footsteps, setting the scene for the perfect attack.

She straightened putting her hands behind her back as he grew closer. "Why would I call you?"

"Because I should have been the one to pick you up. I should have taken you to the shower and brought you back home."

She nodded. "Because you're sleeping with me?"

A smart-mouthed temptress, Trent thought. On fire, he stepped right up to her until her breasts brushed against his chest. She didn't step back but raised her head until their gazes met. "Exactly. And since I'm sleeping with you that makes you my responsibility. The next time you need a ride, the next time you need anything, you call me." He took another step wanting to see if she'd back down. She didn't and his arousal pressed harder against the zipper of his pants.

She stepped into him making sure just about every part of her front rubbed against his. "What if I need something now?"

"I've got exactly what you need now," he stated in a low voice seconds before scooping her up into his arms and heading straight for her building.

She let her head fall back, her hair dangling seductively over his arm. "I can walk, you know."

"I told you before I like the feel of you in my arms."

Wrapping her arms around his neck she buried her face in his chest. "I like the feel of being in your arms."

The second they arrived in front of her door Trent put her down, backed her to the wall and tried to kiss the edges of lust away. He was burning for her, his body so hot he thought for sure he'd go up in flames if he didn't get inside of her right this minute.

Minx that she was Tia molded her body to his, using her hand to cup the nape of his neck, bringing him down, sucking his tongue deeper into her mouth.

"Keys," he growled when he could tear his lips from hers for a second.

"Right," she said out of breath.

He didn't move away from her, loved the feel of her pressed so securely against him. It was then that Trent looked just over her shoulder. Then he saw her door was already ajar.

"Don't move," he told her in a voice that had gone steely.

Tia instantly tensed. He was looking so serious. Deadly serious. "Trent?" she called his name but he didn't look at her again.

Instead he took a step away from her. His big frame was rigid, each movement precise, planned.

She reached out, touched his arm. "What's going on?"

His head snapped back to her. "I said don't move."

She froze, the combination of his voice and his gaze stilling her.

Tia gasped when she saw him reach a hand behind him and come back holding a gun.

"What—"

"Keep quiet and don't move!" he said sternly, then moved through the door.

Her front door that he'd simply pushed open. Why was her door unlocked? Her heart had already been pounding with Trent's kiss and the anticipation of his hands on her naked body. Now, it was pounding from fear.

He'd told her to stay still but there was no way she was standing out in the hallway while he went into her apartment like a Shaft wannabe, prepared to shoot first and ask questions later.

She'd meant to follow quietly behind him but the moment she saw the state of her apartment she'd gasped loudly. Trent turned immediately, scowling at her. He looked as if he were about to say something.

The couch had been ripped to shreds, her lamps tossed on the floor, shattered glass was all over. Her big-screen television had been smashed, the recliner turned over and slashed. It was a mess. With a hand over her heart Tia turned away from the scene in the living room and followed Trent into the bedroom.

He'd already looked around and was moving into the bathroom but Tia stepped through the doorway and stifled another gasp. While the living room was a shock, it was nothing compared to her bedroom. All her clothes were strewn over the floor, the mirror on her dresser was smashed. Her mattresses were turned over and cut so that the springs were now showing.

"Who…who…" she was trying to speak when Trent came up behind her, touching a hand to her shoulder.

"Just breathe," he told her while his fingers massaged her shoulders. "That's right, take slow, deep breaths."

His touch, the fact that he was the one here with her did wonders to calm her racing heart. She'd closed her eyes as she breathed but the scene was clear in her mind.

"Who did this?" she asked in a voice that still sounded shaky.

"I don't know but you better believe I'm going to find out."

An hour later Trent stood in the hallway with Devlin Bonner, Navy SEAL and captain of Trent's team.

"It looks personal," Devlin told him solemnly.

Trent nodded. He'd called his captain before the local police because he'd wanted a like mind to assess the situation. Cops weren't trained the way he and Devlin were. Besides, Trent had sensed this was a personal, not random, attack on Tia when he'd seen her tires this morning.

"She got any enemies?" Devlin stood with his big muscled arms folded over his equally defined chest. He wore a black T-shirt that fit him like a second skin, and jeans that had clearly seen better days. On one hip he had a scabbard with a knife as big and lethal looking as Rambo's. On the other, his gun was holstered. With his dark skin, bald head and the jagged scar running down the left side of his face, he looked dangerous, even scary to someone who wasn't used to seeing him.

To Trent it was the norm; the only reason he didn't look the same was because it would scare his mother to death to see him that way. So when he was home he made a concerted effort to appear as normal as possible. But the lethalness was there always, brimming just beneath the surface of his personality. Today it was about to break free.

"She's pretty famous around here and her pictures are everywhere," he said grimly.

Devlin nodded. "I thought she looked familiar. She's a model, right?"

"Yeah, Tia St. Claire."

"Dayum, she's fine as hell, especially in person," Devlin said with a wide grin.

"Don't even think about it, Bonner." That's what the team called him when they weren't on assignment, because Devlin's mind had one mission when it came to women: hot sex and lots of it.

"Why?" Devlin looked momentarily confused. "Don't tell me you've claimed her already? Trent, you are the man!" Devlin said clapping him on his shoulder. "You haven't been back in town two months and you've already snagged a woman."

Trent didn't like the way "snagged a woman" sounded and immediately grew defensive. "It's not like that. And now's not the time."

Devlin hadn't lost his defensive stance, nor his fierce look, his grin and the slight change in tone was something only Trent would have noticed. The police officers now going in and out of Tia's apartment were still sure to steer clear of them both.

"So since this is personal for you, I'll look into it," Devlin told him.

Trent looked at his commander with nothing short of fury in his gaze. "I want to know who did this and I want his neck in my hands. Do you understand?"

Devlin nodded. "I got it. You just stick close to her. If

they started with her car then moved into her place within the span of a day, they're really gunning for her."

That's exactly what Trent was afraid of.

In her bedroom, or what was left of it, Tia gathered what she could with shaky hands. Tears clouded her eyes as she tried valiantly to keep from shaking. Most of her clothes had been destroyed by what appeared to be hot wax drippings. The furniture was history. But that wasn't what had her so close to a complete breakdown.

The mere thought that someone had been in her house, touching her things, was incomprehensible. She'd had model friends who'd picked up stalkers along their travels. Some who'd had to resort to getting restraining orders because the stalker had shown up at their house. Never had any of her friends had someone actually break into their house.

Turning once more and glancing at her surroundings, Tia gasped. Then, with a knuckle to her lips, she stifled the cry she longed to release. She wasn't alone. If she cried out someone would surely hear her and come running, ready to kill. Someone like Trent. She'd put him through enough already. So much so he probably thought she was a basket case. So it was with all the bravado Tia could muster that she prepared to leave this room and her apartment.

Making her way into the living room, one lone duffel bag in hand, Tia shifted her thoughts to which hotel she'd stay at while she searched for a new place to live. No way was she ever coming back here. She was a little shocked to see that the police had cleared out along with Trent.

She'd wondered where he'd gone when the man he'd introduced as his team captain had shown up, but sensed he wasn't in the mood for questions. Trent's team captain, Devlin Bonner, who to Tia looked more like the human version of Darth Vader, had not returned with him. Now Trent looked even angrier than he had when they'd first come into the apartment together, if that was possible.

His dark eyes had lowered to mere slits, his lips stretched over his teeth on what looked like a naturally fixed scowl. This was the soldier, the man who went into battles for his country. The body that she'd found attractive had morphed into one of a conditioned fighter. His arms seemed bigger, biceps bulging, stretching the rim of the cream colored polo shirt he wore. His jeans fit him just a bit snugger around the thighs, as if all muscles in his body were now more pronounced, more visible for intimidation purposes.

He looked huge and deadly as he marched toward her and for a moment she was afraid of him. She took a step back while keeping her eyes on him. Then, as if he'd sensed her leeriness, he stopped, took a deep breath, then walked toward her again.

Lifting a hand to her chin he asked, "Are you okay?"

Nervously Tia licked her lips, her hands clutching her bag a little tighter. "Yes," she said slowly. "Are you?"

"No," he replied simply. "But I will be once I get you out of here."

He took her by the arm as gently as he possibly could. Tia sensed it was a struggle for him to hold on to his anger while in her presence. She wanted to soothe what looked like an impossible battle in him but wasn't quite sure how to go about it.

"If you could just drop me off at a hotel I'll be all right," she was saying as they walked across the room. He hadn't released her arm and with her words his fingers grew a bit tighter.

"A hotel? Forget it. You're staying with me," he said in a tone that was supposed to brook no argument.

"No!" she said suddenly. Staying in the same house with Trent was not an option. Last night in his arms had pushed buttons she'd rather not admit she had. There was no way she could spend an endless number of nights with him. That wasn't the scope of their relationship. "I mean, I'd rather stay at a hotel," she said calming her voice a bit.

It was only going to make matters worse if she started yelling. Trent was in a precarious state right now, Tia was sure arguing with him wasn't the smartest thing for her to do. But neither was setting up house with him.

Her cell phone rang and she sighed with relief as he released her arm so she could reach into her purse and answer it.

"Hi, Camille," Tia said giving Trent an apologetic look.

"Are you okay? I was so worried about you. Where are you? I keep calling your house but I'm not getting an answer," Camille talked fast as if she were running a race for words.

"I'm at my apartment. You're not getting an answer because the wires were cut," Tia said and instantly regretted her words. Camille was already worried about her. Telling her about the break-in would probably incite a nervous breakdown.

"Oh, my God! Are you serious? Did you call the police? I'm on my way right now!"

"No!" Tia was shaking her head. "It's not necessary for you to come over, Camille. I'm actually on my way out. My stuff is pretty much destroyed so I'm going to find a hotel, then try to regroup."

"You will not stay in a hotel! I'm coming to get you, you can stay here with me."

Tia was officially caught between a rock and a hard place. On the one end there was Trent, still scowling at her, just waiting for her to finish with this call so he could demand she stay with him. Hell, with the way he was looking at her he seemed more inclined to ditch the words and toss her over his shoulder, taking her to his place kicking and screaming.

On the phone was Camille, sweet, delicate Camille who was now screeching like a mother whose child had been in a fight. Choosing the lesser of two evils and the safest option for her own sanity, Tia sighed. "Thanks, Camille. I would love to come stay with you until I find another place."

Chapter 13

Trent seethed all the way over to Camille and Adam's house.

Hadn't he told her she was staying with him? What part of that had she not understood? As angry as he was Trent was not a fool. If he didn't deliver Tia to Camille's front door within the hour she and Adam would both come looking for him. Because in their minds he was the big bad wolf and Tia was their precious Li'l Red Riding Hood.

Never before had his reputation been such a thorn in Trent's side. If they only knew that this time, he wasn't the dangerous one. It was Tia and the effect she had on him. On more than one occasion he'd asked himself why he was even bothering with her. What made her so different that he'd change all the habits he'd had where women were concerned? He still didn't have those answers and at this moment didn't care to think about it.

There were more pressing matters on his mind, like

who the hell had targeted Tia and why? Now, that was a part of his personality that wasn't about to change any time soon. The protective part, the part that would bring down such vengeance on anyone who dared to mess with his loved ones.

Right now the rage moved through him steadily, like lava pouring down the side of a volcano. The slashed tires and then the break-in, hell yeah, he was poised and ready to strike at the next target in a heartbeat.

The moment they arrived and he parked the car she was reaching for the door handle, trying, he knew, to get away from him as fast as she could. He'd scared her when he'd called in Devlin and barked orders to the local police. That much was clear by the way she'd moved away from him, being careful to keep her distance.

He reached for her arm, preventing her exit. "Look, I don't like this situation. I especially don't like that you're not going to be close enough for me to protect."

She gave him a look that said she was about to tell him he didn't need to protect her. She looked so sexy when she defied him that Trent almost let her go ahead and say it. But that would only make him want to throw her in the backseat and ravage her. That would never do, especially since out of the corner of his eye he could see Camille opening the front door and running down the couple of steps in the front of their house toward his truck.

"Don't say anything, Tia," he said, his voice lowering. "Just be careful." He gritted his teeth. "Until I get to the bottom of this, I want you to be very careful. Can you do that? For me? For yourself?" he asked, finally loosening his grip so that his fingers were sliding along the smooth skin of her arm instead of gripping her.

She sighed, then the corners of her lips lifted in a smile.

The smile that he knew had never appeared in any of her pictures, that personal smile that Trent wanted to keep all to himself. "I'll be careful, Trent. I promise."

Then Camille was at the door wrenching it open and hugging Tia even before she could step down from the truck. Trent shook his head then got out on his side only to meet Adam head on. He and his little brother had been having a hard time coming to terms with the role Tia was playing in Trent's life. Trent knew why; he knew Adam's worries were centered around Camille. He wanted to tell him that he had no plans to hurt Tia, then again, he wanted to tell him to mind his damned business.

In the end he simply pulled him to the side. "Look, I've called Devlin in, we're going to investigate the tire slashing and the break-in. I need you to keep a close eye on Tia while she's here."

For a moment Adam simply stared at him strangely.

"Did you hear what I said?" Trent asked, uncomfortable with Adam's glare but knowing he had more pressing issues at hand.

"Yeah," Adam nodded. "I hear you."

Trent looked over to Tia, whom Camille was now escorting up the walkway. Camille was treating her as if she were a fragile toy that was on the verge of breaking. When Tia looked over her shoulder and found his gaze, Trent realized he wanted to treat her that way, too. He wanted to hold her and to protect her from all hurt and danger.

"Are you okay?" Adam was saying.

"What? Oh, I'm fine. I just want to find out what's going on. Camille hasn't gotten any fan mail or anything for Tia at the office, has she?"

"Not that I know of. When she told me about the

break-in this morning I started thinking the same thing. A stalker maybe."

"That's plausible since she's in the spotlight all the time. She didn't seem to think they'd taken anything from her apartment. Not that she had much there to start with. I don't think she wants a home, Adam. She's just existing, not really living."

"Because of the accident?"

Trent nodded. "I'm hoping she'll let Camille find her some help. You know, someone to talk to, like a therapist."

"That's providing she'll tell Camille what happened. Camille said she's known for a while that there was something going on with Tia but that Tia wouldn't open up to her. It's been hell trying to keep this from her."

"But I appreciate you doing it. I didn't want Tia to know I'd checked out her background, let alone told you and Linc about it." Trent sighed. "I've got a feeling Tia isn't going to have a choice but to tell Camille now. She's pretty persuasive, that woman of yours, and the way she just huddled Tia off, she's not going to stop until she knows everything."

Adam chuckled. "You're probably right."

Trent turned and headed back to the truck.

"Where are you going? Aren't you going to come inside and be with Tia?"

"No." Trent answered simply.

"Come on, man. She's obviously shaken up." Adam had walked to the truck with him.

"And she's obviously in good hands with Camille." Opening the door and getting in, Trent sighed, then looked over to his brother and his disapproving glare. "Look, Adam, I can't be the charming hero like you. I'm not the smooth champion like Linc. I need to do what I do best."

"And what's that, leave?"

"No. Fight."

*   *   *

"You have to know it's not your fault, Tia." Beverly Donovan took her hand as they sat on the couch in Camille's Parisian-inspired living room. What looked like a picture right out of an extreme homes magazine with its warm golden walls, crown molding, high ceilings and amber lighting was quite comfortable.

Camille had given Tia enough time to take a bath and eat a delicious brunch before Beverly and Noelle arrived and the interrogation began. It was a good thing she'd already decided not to even fight this battle. As much as she hated to admit it, Trent had been right, it was past time she started living again. And the first step to that was to be honest with the person who seemed to be more in her corner than Tia realized.

Never having had a best friend, Camille Davis was quickly fitting the bill with her. For months she'd been right there, not only offering Tia jobs, but offering her support. In that smart, subtle way that was pure Camille-like, the extraordinary fashion designer had been, as Tia realized today, waiting for the moment Tia cracked and told her about what was going on.

Tia hadn't anticipated doing so in front of Beverly and Noelle but found it didn't bother her as much as she'd thought. Noelle had been quick to inform her that Jade would have been here had Linc not locked her in her room to get some rest after all the festivities yesterday. She completely understood and vowed to call Jade personally to apologize for adding the drama to her baby shower.

"On some level I knew it wasn't my fault. I wasn't driving the car and I wasn't driving the truck that distracted Jake," Tia said. "Still, I was the only one who survived."

"There's a reason for that," Beverly told her. "The Lord doesn't make any mistakes."

Tia smiled. "That's exactly what my mother says."

"Then she's a very smart woman and I fully intend to meet her sometime soon." Beverly kept rubbing the back of Tia's hand. "Making yourself sick with grief is a slap in the face to the memory of Jake and Jessica and I know that's not what you want to do. You're a beautiful young woman with your entire life ahead of you, Tia. I'm not even going to sit by and let you shut yourself away because you think that's what you deserve."

Across the room Camille nodded. "And neither am I."

Noelle, who had just finished her second Mojito, a drink which she swore was too light to be considered alcohol and hence her reasoning for having it with brunch instead of the orange juice Camille had and the Bloody Mary Beverly was still working on. "I guess I'll have to take you out partying to get you back in the swing of things," she said with her leg draped over the back of the truffle colored settee in the corner.

"Thanks," Tia said, so overwhelmed by the support shown to her by these women who barely knew her that tears glazed her eyes. "But first I think I'm going to take a piece of advice offered to me this morning."

"What advice is that?" Camille asked.

"To get the name of your therapist and pay her a visit or two."

Camille came to sit on the other side of Tia. "Oh, that's a great idea. I'll get it for you. She's terrific. Once you get all this out you'll feel so much better."

"I'm curious," Beverly said as she leaned forward to pick up her drink and take a sip. "Who gave you this fabulous advice?"

That had Tia sighing. "I guess I shouldn't have said it was advice. It was almost in the form of a threat."

Noelle threw her head back and laughed. "Then I know where it came from. None other than Trent with his domineering military mentality."

Camille rolled her eyes. "Please tell me he hasn't been browbeating you."

Tia felt her cheeks heat with embarrassment. Did the light spankings he gave while they were in the throws of passion count as browbeating? She cleared her throat.

"He's definitely doing something to me," she said without another thought. The question now was what she planned to do about it.

Linc and Adam were looking at each other conspiratorially. Trent tried to ignore them, he didn't have time for their antics right now. He'd gone over the folder he had with Tia's personal information in it twice since arriving back at his place earlier this afternoon. He'd stopped by her apartment once more just in time to see the police wrapping up. Taking the lead investigator's name was just a formality, Trent had every intention of investigating this matter himself.

Nothing in her file indicated that she'd ever had a stalker. But that didn't mean there wasn't one out there. Trent had seen this all before, someone totally obsessed with someone else until all rational thought simply fled from their mind. And with Tia's visibility there could be any number of suspects running around.

That's exactly why this impromptu visit from his brothers was inconvenient. He wanted to spend his time solving it, not rehashing it over tea. Not that Donovan men ever drank tea.

"What do you two want?" he said going back to his desk and taking a seat at his computer.

"See I told you he's crabby," Adam said nudging Linc.

The brothers moved closer to the desk. "Trent's always crabby, Adam," Linc said looking closely at his younger brother.

"What is up with you two and these female terms? Crabby? I'm a guy, I'm not crabby."

"Then let's just say you're in a foul mood," Adam suggested.

"Let's just say I'm pissed off because some nutcase has decided to make Tia his target. Slashing her tires wasn't good enough, he had to go one step further by invading her privacy."

"This kind of stuff happens every day, Trent," Linc pointed out.

"That doesn't make it right."

"No. It doesn't. But I don't recall you getting this worked up about it, either."

Looking over at the two of them Trent sighed. In his haste to get rid of them he'd been talking directly into their trap. "I'm a military man, any type of injustice bothers me. That it happens to be someone I know just makes it worse."

Linc sat on the edge of the desk looking down at him. "And that it happens to be the woman you're sleeping with makes it…what? Personal?"

"It makes it important."

Linc raised a brow.

"All right, it's personal!" Trent yelled sitting back so that his chair leaned with him. "She doesn't need anything else on her mind right now. I'm trying to get her to see a therapist about her grief issues. I don't want her to hurt any more than she already is."

"And there you have it," Adam said to Linc. "Just like I told you."

Linc nodded while Trent looked from one of them to the other. "What are you talking about?"

"You're in love with Tia," Linc said simply.

"What? Hell, no!" he said jumping up out of his chair. "I'm a Donovan, remember? The last one standing as I recall."

"The last one to fall, I believe," Adam said with a grin spreading across his face.

"You're crazy. I'm not in love with her or anyone else. I don't do love and relationships."

"And why is that, Trent? You never really told us," Linc questioned. "I mean, we all had our issues with relationships but you've always gotten what you wanted out of them. I don't ever recall you having a broken heart or going through any type of drama over a female. So what gives with the no-commitment routine?"

Dragging a hand over his face Trent realized that it was either talk to them now or talk to them and his mother later. Because if Adam and Linc thought he was in love there was no doubt they were ready to spread the word and Beverly Donovan would be the first person they'd go to.

She'd already called him from Camille's house just before Tia had finished with her bath. He had a confirmed lunch date with her tomorrow afternoon and he already knew what the topic of discussion was.

"Look, I can't be in love with anyone. What's the point?"

"What's the point in being in love?" Adam asked and shrugged his shoulders. "Contentment. Satisfaction. Partnership."

"And unlimited sex that goes beyond any casual encounters you've ever experienced," Linc chimed in. "That's a stupid question. We're grown men, the rules we made for ourselves years ago don't and shouldn't apply anymore. All of us are

more than capable of having long lasting, fulfilling relationships. Adam and I have found it, so what's your problem?"

Trent moved to the window and fiddled with the handle
that would open and close the blinds. "I wasn't looking for
love," he said solemnly.

Adam sighed. "Neither were we. But we weren't stupid
enough to turn it away when we found it. Well, at least I
wasn't," he said smiling over at Linc.

Trent had to chuckle at that. Jade had come back into
Linc's life by way of a debt her sister, Noelle, owed to his
casino. In an attempt to work that debt off, she'd ended up
losing even more money to Linc's gaming tables. The two
of them had been involved briefly in college but the
moment he realized who she was, he knew he wanted
another chance with her, so he'd offered her an ultima-
tum—be his date for a week during the Donovan family
reunion, or be prosecuted for the full amount she and her
sister now owed to the Gramercy. In the end Linc fell in
love and instead of professing his love to Jade, he'd attempted to make another deal with her. Unfortunately, Jade
wasn't one to make deals on love. Now look at them,
happily married, with twins on the way.

"I don't begrudge either of you your happiness. It's just
not for me. It can't be."

"Why?"

"Because of what I do. I'm not into real estate and I
don't own a casino. I don't wake up every morning, get
dressed and leave for the office only to return at dinner-
time to be with the family."

"So this is about your job with the special ops team?"
Linc asked.

"It's about not knowing if I'll return from a mission
standing tall or in a pine box."

The room was quiet and Trent turned to face his brothers. "Every time I leave for an assignment I watch Mom looking at me with that sadness just etching her eyes. I know that she worries every day I'm away because I can read it in her letters. Dad worries but he's always let me do what was necessary for me. You guys are just you and you respect my choices. But each day I'm away, fighting, I think of you and the impact my death might have on you. Not in the conceited way, but it's tough knowing that my occupation could cause any of you pain." He sighed. "And if I fall in love and marry a woman and start a family, I'm putting them in the same predicament."

"Wow," Adam stated. "That's heavy. I never knew you felt that way."

Trent gave a half smile. "I know. You just thought I was this rough and tough soldier who didn't give a damn about anyone but himself."

"Nah." Adam shook his head. "That's not what I thought, either. You're my brother and I've always looked up to you. The way you knew exactly what you wanted and you did it no questions asked. I just didn't realize what you were giving up to be that way."

"Trent, man, we accept you and your career choice because we know it's important to you. But that doesn't mean you can't have a full life because of it. The woman you chose to be with, if she loved you in return, would accept you just as we have."

"But that would be one more person I'd hurt."

"What if you're hurting her now by not admitting you love her? Did you think of that?"

"It doesn't matter," Trent said finally. "She's not in love with me. She's perfectly content just sleeping together."

Adam laughed and Trent glared at him. His brother always found something funny.

"If that's what you think then I'm going to stop looking up to you. I watched the two of you at Camille's party and then again at the shower yesterday. And I saw you in the truck this morning. Tia's not content with just sleeping with you and I don't care if that's what her mouth says."

Linc nodded. "I have to agree with him, Trent. Maybe you can't see it because up until now you haven't wanted to see it."

That could definitely be true. But Trent had known from the start that Tia wasn't like the other women. He'd known the moment he first kissed her that she had a power over him, a power that he would never willingly give to another. His brothers were right, he was most likely in love with her. He couldn't be sure because this feeling was still foreign to him, but he wasn't stupid by a long shot. There was something going on between the two of them, something more serious than the "lovers only" agreement they'd made.

On the desk his phone rang. Adam answered it.

"It's Devlin," he said handing the phone to Trent.

Trent went to the phone. "What'd you find out?" he asked immediately.

Devlin answered without pause, this was the way they worked. "Interestingly enough there's a security camera at the front entrance to the apartment complex. But there's no on-duty guard and no secured entrance, go figure. Anyway, I got a copy of the tapes from the last week. Looked at the one from last night and the previous night first. A blue sedan with a female driver came in and out both times. Now, normally I'd chalk this up to a resident except for the hours she came in and out—in at nine-forty-seven Friday night and out at three-sixteen, and in at two-ten on Saturday and out at three-thirty."

"Okay," Trent spoke as he ran the times through his head. He'd gone to Tia's place at about nine-thirty on Friday, he remembered because they'd been eating pizza at close to eleven after their romp in the bedroom. He'd left around three because she hadn't wanted him to stay all night. A fact that had bothered him at the time so he was pretty pissed off when he was leaving. Still, if there'd been a car in the parking lot that hadn't been there when he pulled up Trent was sure he would have noticed it.

"During those hours on Friday she could have easily slashed the tires. And the hour she was there on Saturday coordinates with the exact time you said Adam picked Tia up and took her to the baby shower."

"And she never returned from the baby shower, but the assailant wouldn't have known she wasn't coming back." He was rubbing his hand over his head. "They would have had to know about the shower specifically. About Jade and the babies." His stomach twisted with the implications.

"Right," Devlin agreed. "They knew the duration of the baby shower and was sure to get in and out in that timeframe."

"So we're looking at a woman who not only knows Tia, but knows my family." Either factor was cause to have Trent's mind numbing with rage.

"Bingo. I'm about to go over the tapes for the entire week. I've sent the first two over to Josh to magnify the images and get me a name. I just wanted to let you know where we stood."

"Good. Thanks, Dev."

"There's another reason I called, Trent."

Pinching the bridge of his nose Trent wondered if things could get any worse. "Go ahead."

"While I've been in here looking at these tapes I got a call from Troupe."

Yeah, they'd gotten worse. "And?"

"And we ship out on Saturday. Clobol has been spotted in Dubai. They want us to bring him in."

Trent's entire body stiffened. The government had been searching for Johansen Clobol, a reported player in one of the largest terrorist organizations in the Middle East. If they had a positive ID on him they would want him brought in ASAP.

Going to the Middle East now was not in Trent's plans. Then again, he wasn't altogether sure what his plans were. Only a few minutes ago he'd admitted that what he felt for Tia went way beyond the normal flirt, sex and goodbyes. Wasn't this the exact situation he'd been afraid of? Leaving a woman he cared deeply for to enter into a life-threatening situation…a situation he might not return from.

"You still there, man?" Dev asked.

Trent let out the breath he hadn't been aware he was holding. "Yeah. I'm here. Did you call the rest of the team?"

"I told Josh when I called him about the tapes. I'm going to call Red and Baywatch when I hang up with you. I'll send them down tonight to scope things out and set up. Josh and I will go on Tuesday. You can follow up on Saturday."

Trent frowned. "That's not how we usually roll."

"One of us isn't usually distracted, either," Devlin answered quickly. "Look, take care of this situation with your woman first or you'll be worthless to us. It seems pretty cut-and-dry stalker-type actions. When Josh gets us a name we'll pick the crazy chick up and you can pack up and head out. Deal?"

Already being involved with Tia was impacting his career. Or was it his career impacting being involved with Tia?

"Deal. Call me as soon as you get new info."

"You know it."

Hanging up the phone, Trent sat down in the chair, resting his elbows on his knees.

"What's going on?" Linc asked.

Trent wanted to answer that question, he wanted to tell his brothers everything but on the coffee table his cell phone vibrated.

Linc picked it up and handed it to Trent. It was a text message from Sam Desdune.

Been trying to call you. Left two voice messages last night. Larice Summerfield is missing.

Trent re-read the message then cursed, throwing the phone across the room.

Chapter 14

Adam and Camille had a great home gym. It had been two days since Tia had moved into their home. That meant two days of spending the day at the office with Camille and the nights having dinner with first Jade and Noelle and then with Camille and Adam.

Normally this would have made Tia feel crowded and anxious, instead she'd felt more rested and serene than she had in months. It may have been due to the king-sized four-poster bed in the guest room that Camille had put her in. Still, keeping with her less-is-more theme, Tia had decided she was definitely indulging in a bed like that when she found her new place.

That had been one of the thoughts on her mind in the past two days: where she would move to? She'd called Camille's therapist, Jeanne Brokeman, yesterday and had her first appointment this afternoon. In her estimate it hadn't gone too badly. Jeanne was a small woman with a very low-key demeanor. She spoke in an almost hushed tone that Tia swore therapists and psychiatrists perfected. Her office had a comfortable feel with warm colors like champagne and beige and cranberry throughout its décor. And talking to her hadn't been as difficult as Tia had thought.

The session had ended and Tia had checked her cell phone the moment she'd left the office.

Trent still hadn't called.

It was silly, she knew. She should just call him. But, truth be told, the other Donovans had been keeping her so busy the last two days that she hadn't really had an opportunity. And if she wanted to be even more honest with herself, she would admit that she was afraid to talk to him.

No matter how much she craved his touch, his overbearing remarks or even that contemplative look he gave her when he thought she wasn't watching, she was still scared. She'd warned herself before becoming involved with him and so thought she'd been well prepared, just as she'd thought she was dealing with her grief issues in the right way.

Trent was too much for her. There was no way she could have resisted him or the threat he was to her heart. Yes, the physical had crossed over to emotional the night he'd held her in his arms without making love to her. He'd been caring and sympathetic, all the while holding his ground. He knew about the accident because he'd had her investigated. Tia still didn't know what to make of that. Did he investigate every woman he slept with or did this somehow make her special?

Still, he'd known and he hadn't said anything to her about it. Maybe he was respecting her privacy, but then if that were the case he wouldn't have snooped into her background in the first place. At any rate, the secret was now out and everybody, including her mother, was glad of it. It wasn't as if she were a murderer and Tia admitted it felt better to not walk around holding something in all the time.

Except now she was holding something entirely different inside. Another thought that had plagued her for the past two days.

She wanted Trent Donovan. No, she really wanted him and not just in her bed. Now how stupid was that? She'd gone this long in her life and had made one major reconciliation with herself at the same time dooming her heart to endless pain and suffering.

Trent wasn't the settle-down type of man. She'd known that before sleeping with him and while he didn't remind of her of that fact, she knew it just the same. She'd thought she could stick with just having sex with him. Now she wasn't quite sure. He had proven to be more caring and tender with her than anyone she had ever known.

In Adam and Camille's home gym, she used her favorite method to clear her mind. Sitting on the bench she did sets of fifteen with the ten-pound free weights. She was on her fourth set of ten when she felt a warmth at her back.

Before she could turn around to surmise what it was his lips were on her neck, his hands sliding down her arms to her wrists where he continued the motion of her lifting the weights.

Speak of the devil.

He'd waited as long as humanly possible, giving her the time and space Linc said she probably needed. A lot had happened in her life since Saturday and while it was Trent's way to make a bold presence he adhered to his big brother's advice and left her alone.

But he'd ached for her. The last two nights alone in his

bed had been torture. There had never been another woman to spend the night in his bed until Tia and now it didn't seem right without her. The fact that he'd been coming to terms with his own feelings for her while following up on her stalker and the case he'd left behind in Connecticut only made seeing her more difficult. Trent made a concerted effort to keep his mind on business—that was the only way he could hope to keep Tia safe.

Larice Summerfield was the daughter of Roland Summerfield, the man indicted for attempted murder and a host of other crimes back east.

Trent had gone to help his friend Sam protect the Bennetts, an influential family, and find the person threatening them. Larice had been stalking one of the men in the Bennett family and Trent had been the one to arrest her. Now she was missing.

And Tia was being stalked.

The connection was just farfetched enough to be possible and Sam had arrived in Vegas yesterday to add his input and help into finding the stalker. Devlin had flown out to Dubai earlier this morning. Josh was already there. Now it was up to Trent and Sam to get to the bottom of this. And then he'd be leaving.

Trent didn't want to think of that right now. However, it was just that fact that had him leaving Sam at his condo and riding over here at almost ten at night to see Tia. If he was going to be leaving her in a week, not knowing when or if he would return, he needed to be with her as much as possible.

A couple of weeks ago he'd told her that three days was just too long for them to be apart, now he was thinking that two might be pushing it, as well.

Adam knew what had kept him away just as he knew that Trent would eventually show up at his door. He hadn't said anything when Trent arrived but "She's in the gym."

The brothers had been spending a lot of time together these past two days trying to get a grip on what might be happening with Tia and how it could affect them all. Adam was initially worried about Camille and the backlash CK Davis Designs might have but with the Larice Summerfield connection in the back of all their minds, that seemed less than likely. If Larice were behind the break-in and tire slashing then the blame rested solely on Trent's shoulders.

Guilt, lust, and anxiousness were not a good mixture for a man like Trent. So when he'd walked into the home gym and seen her lifting the free weights, her mind focused, her gaze straight ahead as she breathed with each repetition, he'd become more than aroused.

Like a vice around his heart her presence engulfed him. Tugged and squeezed him until Trent had to struggle to breathe. It was so beyond the way her taut body looked in those tight exercise shorts and even tighter sports bra. Even more than the enticing way her skin shone with the light sheen of sweat she'd worked up. And three times as alluring as the sweep of her hair over the line of her back.

The physical had shifted to emotional as easily as a carefree summer breeze over the trees. He'd avoided this type of connection all his life and now it was here, settled quite comfortably in the pit of his stomach. And just as Trent did with all things in his life, he'd thought about the effect these feelings would have on him, his family and this woman. And determined that no plan of action could have ever prepared him for this. He loved Tia St. Claire regardless of his dangerous job or her troubled past, or even the reputation he'd worked to keep intact.

He wanted to tell her, to see the look on her face when he actually said the words but her back was to him and the need to touch her overwhelmed him. He'd taken slow, measured steps that caused his body to ache even more as he approached her. Straddling the bench he scooted until her body fit perfectly against his, then his lips and his hands did what they'd been craving to for the last two days.

"I'm beginning to think you have a problem with my workout regimen," she said in a shaky voice.

Beneath his hands she trembled, her neck angling to fit against his shoulder as he continued to slide his tongue along the smooth column.

"I have no problems with you at all," he mumbled, then sank his teeth lightly into her skin only to soothe the spot with his tongue once more.

"Really?" she asked and leaned forward to put her weights on the floor. Turning slightly she grasped his chin in her hand. "Well, I have one major problem with you, Trent Donovan."

His body instantly tensed. While the look in her hazel eyes said simply "Take me now," her other features were stern as if she were prepared to scold him.

"I'm a great problem solver," he said, determined that if he wasn't making love to her he'd keep the mood as light as possible.

"Then maybe you can tell me why three days is too long for us to be apart but two seems to be okay."

Yes, he definitely loved this spunky, dangerously beautiful woman.

"Two days are also too long."

She stood then, looking down on him. "Don't let it happen again," she told him, moving his legs so that they were together and she could straddle him.

"Never," he said loving the smooth way in which she positioned him the way she wanted him. His hands quickly went to the delicious curve of her bottom while her arms went around his neck.

Lifting his face to hers he met her kiss, touching his tongue to hers lightly at first, then with more urgency. "I missed you," he groaned as she pressed her body closer to his.

"Not as much as I missed you," she answered.

With a growl his hands came up her torso where he pulled up the rim of her sports bra until her full breasts were bared before him.

"I missed these," he crooned then licked a tongue over one already erect nipple.

"Mmm." She arched her back.

He palmed both globes, loving the feel of their fullness in his hands. Back and forth he paid close attention to each one letting the arousing sounds of pleasure spur him on.

Knowing that would never be enough, Trent slipped a hand down into her shorts, pressing farther until he'd moved past her thong to find the moist haven he'd been looking for. She bucked above him just as his fingers parted her already wet folds.

"I definitely missed this," he groaned, positioning his other hand at the center of her back as she arched again.

"Trent," she sighed, her entire body quivering from his touch.

He drove her hard and fast. She needed release and he desperately wanted to watch her receive it. Her hair hung in its ponytail swaying back and forth as she moved. Her exposed breasts swayed and his mouth watered. Switching from one finger to two he moved deeper inside of her, his mind a complete blur to anything other than this woman, the warm feel of her arousal gripping and coating his fingers. The sound of her voice chanting his name. She was taking him to heights he'd never even imagined.

When her thighs shook on top of his Trent touched his thumb to the tightened nub of her center, applied pressure while his two fingers continued to work her on the inside. She screamed, yes, screamed his name. It sounded so sweet, so blissfully erotic that Trent didn't give a damn if Adam and Camille, who were somewhere in the house, most likely in their own bedroom on the second level, or anyone chancing to drive by the house heard her.

Exhausted from the exertion Tia fell forward, resting her forehead on his shoulder. He held her there, bringing both arms to wrap around her waist.

"I need you," Trent whispered as their hearts beat frantically against each other.

"I'm right here," she said lifting her head to plant butterfly kisses on his forehead, down his cheeks, then over his mouth. "Take me."

Trent needed no further direction.

Standing with her in his arms, he released her so that she slid sinuously down his body. Grabbing the sports bra, he pulled it over her head then bent down, pushing her shorts and her thong down to her ankles while she stepped out of them. On his way back up Trent kissed her calves, her knee caps, her thighs. His lips touched the dark triangle of close cut curls at her juncture whispering erotic compliments over her as he went. Moving upward again he kissed her navel, delving his tongue quickly inside until her hands clenched his head. Continuing, he licked and kissed all along her torso until he was once again at her lovely breasts.

"Beautiful," he whispered. "Sinfully beautiful."

Then he took her mouth in a kiss that left no question of what he wanted, no, needed from her. The way she moved into his embrace, wrapping her arms tightly around his neck said she acquiesced.

In moments Trent had turned her, bending her over to

flatten her palms on the weight bench. His pants and boxers released and fell to his ankles in no time as he positioned himself between her legs and sank his aching arousal firmly, deeply inside of her.

She moved forward, dropped her head and sucked in a breath. He was deeper inside of her than he'd ever been and he knew it was a lot for her to take so he remained still for a moment while she acclimated herself. A second later her hips shifted and Trent gritted his teeth.

He pulled back and thrust inside of her again, choosing a rhythm that both stoked his feral desire and glided along this emotional buildup that threatened to overtake him.

He loved her. Everything about her from her smile to her tears, her laughter to her anger, it was all emblazoned in his mind, finding that place he'd never allowed another woman. He loved being inside of her, touching her so intimately she had no choice but to think of only him.

"Tell me you missed me, baby. I need to hear you say it again."

"Yes, Trent," she panted. "I missed…you…so…much."

His hips moved faster, his fingers gripping her at the hips, holding her still. He couldn't see her face but her hair brushed over her back and he reached forward pulling the band away until it cascaded over her back and off her shoulders. The sight aroused him more, making him need more from her, crave more from her.

Lifting his palm he tapped her lightly on the bottom and was rewarded by a shiver of her entire body. He'd done this before, just a soft tap and she'd responded so deliciously he knew he'd do it again. With the other hand he tapped the other cheek.

Her nails dug into the vinyl of the weight bench, her toes curling as he moved inside her. This position had become a ritual with them, as familiar and essential as breathing. When his palm landed on one cheek she gasped, letting the tiny thrill spikes run rampant through her body.

"More," she groaned.

He smiled.

Tap. Thrust. Tap. Thrust. Tap. Thrust.

On and on until he couldn't hold back any longer.

"Tia!" Her name was a guttural moan ripped from his throat at the same time his essence was milked from his soul.

It was on the tip of his tongue, the words he'd never said to a woman before. He felt it as he leaned forward, holding her tightly. Like a blanket covering them both he felt his feelings evolving, wrapping in the form of his arms around her. He needed this woman more than his career or his bachelor status, more than he needed to breathe.

She needed to know, he needed to tell her. He kissed her shoulder, swallowed and opened his mouth to speak. Then his cell phone rang.

After the interruption of Sam's phone call he and Tia had re-dressed in the gym and gone up to her room to shower. As he'd sat on the bed digesting what he and Sam had talked about combined with these new feelings for her Tia had sat across from him in another chair.

She looked, for the first time since he'd met her, nervous and unsure. When he'd asked what was wrong she'd tried to play it off by changing the subject.

"Who is Sam?" she'd asked.

"A friend of mine from back east. He owns a private investigation firm."

"And he came all the way across the country to help you run down a stalker?"

Trent shrugged. "When I left a couple of months ago I

went to Connecticut to help Sam with a big case he had going on. I guess he's just repaying the favor."

"Camille told me about that case. It was pretty big and dangerous, she said." She'd lifted her legs in the chair, wrapping her arms around them.

She looked like a frightened child and Trent's heart hurt for all the turmoil she was going through.

"Nothing I haven't seen before."

"Is that the way you felt about his sister?" she asked, startling Trent. "That she was nothing you haven't seen or done before?"

Wow, he'd never had to justify his actions to another woman. Hell, he'd never justified them to anyone. There was no question how she'd found out about Lynn—from Camille. Adam would not have wasted any time telling his wife about it. No wonder the two of them were so convinced that he was up to no good with Tia.

Still, there was no doubt that Trent would make Tia understand the differences between her and Lynn Desdune and all the other women he'd been with.

Leaning forward with his arms resting on his knees, he looked at he intently. "Lynn and I were attracted to each other. We acted on that attraction. At no time were there serious feelings involved." But being with Lynn and her son had started him wondering about a family of his own.

She nodded but Trent couldn't tell if that was a good or bad thing. "She has a son?"

"Yes. She has a son and he's a great kid. Whatever you've heard," he began honestly, "know that I don't play with people's emotions. Lynn and I both knew the score. Every woman I've ever been involved with has always known my limitations, otherwise I don't get involved at all."

"Your limitations? So you never intend for anything serious to develop from your relationships?"

Trent heaved a sigh. She was right on target, but the words coming from her mouth made him feel lower than dirt. Still, he'd opted to take the honest route—there was no use stopping now. "No. It was just about sex."

For a moment she'd looked shocked and Trent wondered what he could come up with to fix whatever he'd said that was wrong. Then her lips had spread into a nervous smile and she'd released her legs to stand. Holding her hand out to him, she led him back to the bed. "I'm tired, let's get some sleep," she'd said.

Still baffled Trent wasn't sure what to do but he stood and walked around to the side of the bed with her. She pulled back the sheets and he stopped her.

"That first night you wanted me to stay with you because it was the anniversary that you didn't want to relive alone."

She nodded. "Yes. Having you there made the bad dreams go away." Looking up at him, she smiled again, tentatively. "You're a hero, even in dreams."

Trent lifted a hand to her cheek, cupping her face. She turned in slightly, kissing his palm. "The other nights you sent me home."

She closed her eyes and for endless moments they stood there just like that.

When she opened them again it was with some semblance of resignation. "And tonight I'm asking you to stay."

"Is there any particular reason for that?" Trent asked, for the first time wondering about Tia's feelings for him. She'd asked about Lynn almost as if she were jealous or hurt by the thought of him with another woman. But then she'd let the subject drop like yesterday's news.

"I'm tired of being alone, Trent," she'd said simply, those luminescent eyes weaving a tight noose around his heart.

And so he'd stayed.

He'd slept in that bed beside her, holding her, watching her as she slept, wondering what he'd ever done in his life to deserve her.

"Good morning," Camille said as she walked into the kitchen the next morning.

She didn't look too surprised to see him at her kitchen table at a little after eight in the morning, having a humongous bowl of cereal. Trent assumed Adam had told her he was there last night.

"You're out of Cap'n Crunch," he said to Camille as she moved from one part of the kitchen to the next, opening and closing cabinets to put a pot of coffee on.

"Then you can go to the store and get some," she quipped. "You would think that you and your brother would have a wider range when it came to your breakfast food. I swear Adam goes through about four boxes of that cereal each week."

Trent laughed. He and Adam used to fight over the last bowl like it was a gold coin. Then his mother would patiently come in from the pantry carrying another box and end their momentary war. Linc was an oatmeal man, which disgusted Adam and Trent, so he was never a part of their cold cereal wars.

"I have to meet with Sam in an hour then I'll be back later to pick Tia up for dinner. I'll be sure to have a box of cereal with me when I return."

Closing the refrigerator, Camille took the seat across from Trent, said her grace and stuck a fork into a thick slice of cantaloupe. Chewing the fruit she watched him contemplatively.

Trent sensed what was coming next but continued to eat the last remnants of his cereal.

"So what are your intentions toward Tia now?"

Good ole Camille. She was a nurturer by impulse. Despite the tumultuous childhood she'd endured, she was hell-bent on taking care of anyone and everyone around her. Anyone and everyone she cared about.

"I want to keep her safe," he answered, knowing it wasn't going to be enough.

"And after you've caught the bad guy?" She speared a piece of watermelon this time and stuck it into her mouth.

To anyone just walking into the room they looked like two normal family members having breakfast. But Trent knew things were on shaky ground with him and Camille, since she'd been a little at odds with him getting involved with Tia. Camille was putting her cards on the table and how he played the hand she dealt him would dictate their relationship from this point on. He immediately thought of Adam and how much his brother loved this woman. Then, he thought, with a warm feeling how much he cared about this woman. In two months she was going to be his sister-in-law, but right now, at this very moment she was like blood kin. And as such he would not lie to her nor would he do anything to purposely hurt her. Of that there was no doubt.

"After I've caught the bad guy I want to see where things can go with us." He raised a hand to stop her next words. "No, not like that. It's more than just sex now, Camille. It's much more."

She was chewing a grape then and she dropped her fork, letting it clink against the glass bowl as she sat back in her chair. "I can't believe it," she said, narrowing her eyes to look at him.

"You can't believe what?"

She chuckled softly. "Jade said it would hit you hard. That it would shock you right along with the rest of us."

"What are you talking about? What's hit me hard?"

"You're in love with her, aren't you?"

She was staring at him, not that it made him uncomfortable, but he was getting tired of admitting this to everyone except the person whom he needed to hear it most. Lifting his bowl, he drank the milk then put it back down. Using the napkin she'd tossed at him, he wiped his mouth, then sat back in his chair similar to the way she was.

"Yes, I'm in love with her."

In seconds Camille was up out of her chair coming around to wrap her arms around his neck. "Oh, Trent! That's fantastic! I'm so happy for you two. Tia needs somebody to take care of her although she'd never admit it. And I'm so happy it's you." She pulled away from him then. "Because you need someone to keep you in line and Tia's just the woman to do it."

"Are you making moves on my woman now?" Adam asked half jokingly as he walked into the kitchen.

Camille ran to him hugging him a little tighter, a little more intimately than she'd hugged Trent. "Oh, Adam, he loves her! He told me he loves her."

You would have thought Trent had proposed to Camille the way she bounced happily around that kitchen. Over her shoulder Adam looked at him. His brother's arms had instinctively gone around Camille, holding her close as his lips curled into a smile.

This was what true love looked like. And for the first time in his life Trent envied it. He wanted what his brother had. He wanted a woman to love him this deeply, this unconditionally, that the happiness of his family would inspire her this way.

Last night they'd slept together, but they both must have been extremely tired because all they did was sleep. He'd held her and she'd cuddled against him but neither of them had awakened until he slipped away from her a little over half an hour ago to get ready for his meeting with Sam.

They would talk about this tonight. He had to get his feelings off his chest and he would finally know hers.

Chapter 15

Per Trent's note, which he'd left on the bedside table this morning, Tia was dressed and waiting to be picked up. It was silly, she knew, but the butterflies were having a field day in the pit of her stomach.

Just as he'd said before, she and Trent had moved backward. They'd become lovers before they'd had the chance to date. So tonight would be their first official date. He'd told her to wear something dazzling and that he'd pick her up at seven. It was seven-o-four.

She heard the front door open and close and her heart pounded.

All day she'd thought about Trent, about their tryst in the gym and the night spent in each other's arms. She'd also thought about their conversation about the last woman he'd been with before her.

If nothing else she gave Trent points for being brutally

honest. A lesser man would have tried to convince her that all the other women in his past meant nothing and that there was only her. But Trent hadn't gone that route. Instead he'd answered her questions and let her draw from them what she would. For a moment she thought she saw a shadow of worry in his face and that's when she'd ended the conversation.

She had a life before that fateful night that she and Trent first slept together and she respected that he did, too. Asking him to her bed had been an informed decision. She knew his reputation, knew his kind and that was exactly what she wanted.

At the time, that was exactly what she wanted.

Now was a different story. She'd been only seconds away from confessing her love to him. Just moments away from laying her feelings at his feet, for him to do with what he would. Then she'd stopped, thought better of exposing herself that way and simply asked him to bed. Because that's where she dealt with Trent best, in bed.

Cuddled in his arms in the late hours of the night, she realized that while dealing with him in bed had been easy for her, dealing with the way he filled her heart sure wasn't going to be.

Since she'd just begun therapy sessions with Dr. Brokeman, the doctor wanted to see her as frequently as possible. So she'd gone again this morning, but this time instead of talking about her past she was more concerned with her future.

Tia was no stranger to therapy. For months after the accident she'd seen a shrink. She'd talked to him and tried to get a grip on her emotions. But after a while it just seemed useless. At that point she was determined to live in the bubble of grief she'd created for herself.

Now with new things in her life like the friendship offered by Camille and the Donovans and, of course, Trent, she had begun to think that maybe, just maybe, it was time to move on.

"He's not like any other man I've ever met," she told Jeanne as she sat in the soft leather chair across from where Jeanne sat on the couch.

"Really? How so?"

She'd sighed. "The other men, since Jake, I mean, were happy-go-lucky content with a romp in bed and maybe a movie or dinner. They knew that I was a model and thought this was their key into the fast lane. I always knew that I was a passing fad with them and that we'd eventually part."

"And that was fine with you?"

"It worked for me."

"And now? Does this new man work for you?"

Tia had thought about that question for a moment then exhaled. "I think he does. He's not impressed with what I am, but seems overly concerned with who I am. If that makes sense."

Jeanne nodded. "It does."

"He has his own money, his own life. He knows what he wants and he goes after it. For a while I figured I was just another thing on his want list."

"Did you want to be just another thing on his list?"

"I wanted the pain to go away. And he was there. He came into that room and he was bent on saving me, and whether it was from driving while intoxicated or from the endless pit of despair I was spiraling down didn't matter. He was just there to play the hero role. And he did a damned good job."

"Is he still your hero, Tia?"

She smiled and thought about the baby shower and the break-in at her apartment. "He is. But unlike ordinary heroes I'm not just thankful to him for saving me." She tried to get the words out without sounding too silly. "He's…it's…it's just more than I thought it would be. More than I thought I could feel again."

"Do you think that's good or bad?"

"I think it's about damned time," she said with a release of breath.

So with that said Tia was determined to let Trent know how she felt, to just get it over with. This first date was going to be the time of revelation. Ready or not Trent Donovan was about to get the shock of his life.

Stepping out of the car, Trent passed his keys to the valet and moved around to take Tia's hand. Another valet had helped her out and Trent had been more than disturbed by the way the man's gaze as well as his hands had lingered on her.

Luckily it only took one snarl from him to get him to back the hell up. She'd looked up at him and shaken her head.

"You are so bad. The man was just doing his job."

"Then he can do it with someone else's woman," he'd said without hesitation. Tia was his and that was a fact.

He walked her through the doors of the Paris Las Vegas hotel. The hotel looked like a million bucks and so did he and Tia. She wore a shimmery silver dress with thick straps at her shoulders and a deep V neckline. From her waist down it flared out, moving sinuously over her long legs, tempting and teasing him with every step she took. He'd opted for a tuxedo, black, single breasted Ralph Lauren.

Her arm was entwined with his as they walked and he noticed the men ogling her and pulled her closer.

Tia knew exactly what Trent was doing and felt the need to do a little claiming of her own. She'd been more than pleased with her own outfit—the Vera Wang cocktail dress with its empire waist and jeweled bodice embroidery was a great choice. She'd been photographed in it once and loved the way it's color added sparkle to her eyes.

Trent looked scrumptious. The three-button notch lapel was her favorite style and only added emphasis to his fantastic build. He'd left the vest at home, going for sophisticated defiance with just the tuxedo shirt and long crimson silk tie. The tie accented his smooth chocolate features giving him an air of danger and elegance all at the same time.

Women didn't miss a thing and heads turned as they moved through the ornately decorated gold and cream lobby of the hotel.

They were seated in a booth dead center of the Eiffel Tower Restaurant. Trent had stood beside her as she slipped into the cranberry colored suede lounge before following on her other side. He sat so close to her their sides touched and she trembled.

Looking forward, she was treated to the spectacular view of the Strip. On the ride up Trent had tipped the elevator guy not to point out the Vegas landmarks. This was a part of the tourist treat to the city but since they both lived here it wasn't necessary, and besides, she was too concerned with the erratic beating of her heart to listen to some tour guide.

Like she'd admitted at the house, she shouldn't be this nervous. She had been sleeping with Trent for a month now. They'd done things in the bedroom that Tia had only read about. Yes, Trent Donovan was a force to be reckoned with in and out of the bedroom. So being nervous around him was simply ridiculous. Still, Tia recognized that submitting to his lovemaking expertise and confessing that she was in love with him were two entirely different things.

Tia and Trent shared the grand seafood platter and

talked about their childhoods, career choices and anything other than their current personal feelings.

Trent was charming and good-looking, all the norm. But tonight he seemed just as jittery as she did, even dropping his fork on the floor twice. She couldn't talk, however, because her shaking hands had spilled the first glass of red wine the waiter had brought her. Telling a man she loved him should not be this difficult.

They were waiting for a cup of coffee to be brought to them before leaving when Tia decided she needed to take a breather, pull herself together and get this over with. Either he was going to accept her feelings or he wasn't, whatever, either way she needed to know.

"I'm going to go to the ladies' room," she announced. A few minutes alone and she could gather her strength.

"I thought you were going to break a record," he said, smiling and scooting out of the booth to come around and help her up.

"What does that mean?"

"Women always go to the ladies' room in restaurants. I think it's some type of bathroom fetish you have." He leaned forward and kissed her lightly on the lips as he laughed.

"That is not even funny. Stereotyping us that way," she feigned indignance. "We can't help if we need to freshen up or heaven forbid actually use the facilities."

"Hey," he said, catching her arm as she tried to brush by him. "You don't need to freshen up. You're beautiful just the way you are."

And now she couldn't even fake annoyance. Her smile was inevitable, the warmth radiating up her arm from where he touched her too potent to ignore. Trent Donovan was one smooth character.

Passing through the door to the ladies' room, Tia quickly

found an empty stall. The bathroom was quiet and she finished quickly moving to the sink to wash her hands and refresh her lip gloss. She was just smacking her lips together and dropping the tube into her small purse when another stall door opened.

A woman stepped out, her hair pulled back into a tight ponytail. Tia was only slightly startled since she'd thought she was in there alone. Still, she smiled through the mirror to the other woman and picked up her purse, turning to leave.

She paused at the door when the woman spoke.

"Tia St. Claire."

Turning, Tia looked at the woman more closely, trying to see if she knew her. She was a lighter complexion than Tia's own honey tone, her eyes unusually dark. She wore a pantsuit, not designer but not cheesy, either.

"Do I know you?" Tia finally asked when recollection was not coming back to her.

"No. But I've made it my business to get to know you."

Tia arched a brow. "Really? And why is that?"

The woman had approached her and was now standing about a foot away. "That's what I do when I have a score to settle."

Something about the way the woman looked at her or the predatory way in which she'd approached had Tia's guard up. Her words only confirmed that Tia needed to be prepared for the woman's next words.

Was this her stalker? she thought momentarily.

"And you have a score to settle with me I take it?" The bravado wasn't faked. Tia was a little nervous—she hadn't fought in a ladies' room since high school, but she was no stranger to defending herself, especially from jealous females.

"Not with you personally but since you've plopped

yourself right in the middle, I'll have to make an example of you."

"You slashed my tires and broke in to my apartment," Tia accused.

"And now I'm going to scar that pretty face so he'll know that I mean business," the woman said, then extended her hand, landing a slap against Tia's cheek.

Tia's head snapped back with the force, her teeth clattering as her right ear began to ring. She supposed the question-and-answer session was now over.

In seconds Tia was on her, grabbing the woman's ponytail with one hand and connecting her fist with her jaw with the other. The woman began swinging wildly, screaming as she did. It took some effort for Tia to keep her face from meeting with the woman's vicious nails, but when her hand slapped free of the woman's hair Tia had no other choice but to knock her to the floor.

On top of the woman now, Tia pulled her hair again, using it to slam her head against the floor. The woman's feet kicked up, pounding into Tia's back. Then she got an arm free and a punch slammed into Tia's left cheek, knocking her off balance.

As Tia fell to the floor the woman pushed herself upward, grabbing Tia by the neck. "You're his bitch! He took my lover away from me and I'm going to do the same to him!"

The woman was dragging Tia on the floor and Tia knew her intent was to ram her face into the wall. So she grabbed the woman's legs, threw her off balance and jumped up off the floor when the woman fell back against the sink. Standing now, Tia slammed a fist into the woman's stomach and was about to repeat the action on her face when she heard the door opening.

As Tia's attention was momentarily taken with the person entering the ladies' room, the stalker pulled out of her grasp. But Tia wasn't about to let her go. She reached for her, grabbing the collar of the woman's jacket. She wiggled free, aiming for the door that was now being held wide-open by the screaming patron.

The woman was fast, and Tia's four-inch heels and the swirling material of her dress slowed her down so that she was left holding only the woman's jacket. Still determined to catch her, Tia barreled out of the bathroom only to have strong hands grab her around the waist, pulling her back quickly.

Pandemonium had broken out as there were more screams and people running in her direction. Tia was trying to break free of the stranger's hold when she was lifted off the floor only to be plopped down directly in front of Trent.

"What the hell happened?" he asked.

"It was her! The stalker!" Tia screamed.

From behind she heard a deep male voice. "It's Larice, Trent. I'm going after her."

Tia whirled around toward the voice and saw the back of a tall guy running through the crowd. He was the one who had grabbed her and he knew Trent.

Turning back to her date for the evening with a litany of questions on her tongue, she was silenced by his grave look. It mirrored the one he'd had in her apartment that day after the break-in.

"What's going on, Trent?" she asked in a shaky voice. "Who was that man? And who is Larice?"

In minutes they were at the ground floor of the hotel waiting less than patiently for Adam to arrive. As if he'd read his brother's mind his car skidded to a halt at the front entrance that was now full of police cars and reporters.

Only because he was who he was could Trent keep Tia away from the reporters and the cops' questions. Now he wanted her to get safely home so that he could do his job.

"Let's go," Adam said moving to Tia's side.

Trent had one of her arms and Adam now had the other, moving her quickly toward the car.

Up until this point Tia had been silent, her questions about who Sam and Larice were died quickly when she saw all the police and reporters milling around. But Trent knew that would only last for so long.

She stopped at the passenger door and turned to him. "I'm going back to the house because I know that whatever is going on is serious. But you better not even think about not coming back to explain this all to me. If you do, so help me, I'll be like your worst enemy hunting you down for answers."

Never had Trent heard her speak this way. His already tense body tightened, his fingers clenching at his sides.

"Go home. I'll be there once I've finished."

She stared at him another second, then got into the car. Adam slammed the car door shut.

"What the hell happened?"

"It's the same person who broke into her apartment. Sam's on her trail. I've gotta go," he said then began to move away. Turning back, he said, "Take care of her."

Adam only nodded before moving around his car and getting in.

If anything happened to Tia because of him and his job Trent would never forgive himself.

It had been a long, grueling night. Through the shared tracking device, Sam had given Trent exact directions to where he was following Larice Summerfield. Trent arrived at the motel outside the city limits and Sam already had Larice cuffed and waiting.

"Why would you come here?" Trent asked with barely masked fury. She sat with her back straight on the dingy bed looking at him as if he were the scum of the earth. "Why would you target Tia?"

"What's the matter, Mr. Donovan? Don't like strangers butting into your business?"

"You're not a stranger, you're a psychopath!" Trent roared.

Sam stood. "I've called the police already. She'll be taken to the station, then extradited back to Connecticut."

"I want her charged in Vegas, as well. Vandalism, breaking and entering, assault." He read off the charges.

"And what will that do? Your little girlfriend already knows I've been messing with her because of you. I doubt she's going to want you back now."

Trent stared at her a moment, her eyes were cold as ice, her stance full of anger and vengeance. But there was something else, something he'd been seeing too frequently in women these days. Hurt.

"You're hoping Tia will kick me to the curb the same way Renny did you," he stated simply.

"If you hadn't interfered we'd still be together!"

Trent shook his head. Lorenzo Bennet was an erotic sculptor and heir to the Bennett Industries fortune. Although he was currently engaged to Sabrina Desdune, Sam's twin sister, he at one time had dated Larice. Apparently she'd never let go of her feelings for him.

"He's in love with someone else, Larice. You have to accept that. Causing me or the woman I'm involved with pain won't make Renny come back to you."

"But you should have minded your own business!" she roared, attempting to jump at him.

Beside him Sam moved but Trent held out his hand to stop him. "I did my job. And as long as you continue to stalk and harass people I'll always be there to take you down. There's no two ways about it."

She sobbed then, gut-wrenching soul-shattering tears that seemed to last forever, or at least until the police came. Once again Trent watched her taken into custody. He wondered just how a person got to that desolate place where nothing or no one else mattered beside the one you loved.

Tonight he'd planned to tell Tia he loved her and they'd been distracted. If Larice had been a more dangerous criminal she could have seriously hurt Tia. Catching her in the ladies' room was the perfect opportunity to take her out. While he'd sat at the table drinking coffee and wondering how to accurately word his feelings for her, he could have lost her.

That's how Larice must have felt, Trent thought as he walked slowly through the foyer and up the steps of Adam's house.

If he'd lost Tia there would be nothing else for him, nothing else worthwhile.

Pausing at the door to the guest room he said a silent prayer that this would work out the way he needed it to. He was about to knock but the door swung open and she stood on the other side.

She'd changed into jeans and a T-shirt and moved to the side to let him in.

"Are you okay?" she asked after she'd closed the door.

Trent turned to stare at her. "I'm fine. But what about you?" She had a scratch that stretched from the bottom of her cheek to the center of her neck on the right side. It was red and angry and he wanted to do nothing more than kiss it away.

"Just fine," she quipped with a half smile. "I haven't fought like that in years."

He chuckled nervously. "It's like riding a bike, isn't it?"

Her smile widened. "Yes. It is."

The room grew silent.

"So who is Larice? An old girlfriend?"

How had he known she would think that first?

"Larice Summerfield is a woman I arrested in Connecticut. She was stalking one of Sam's clients and I was responsible for bringing her in." Taking a deep breath Trent sat on the edge of the bed. "I guess she felt like I'd ruined her chances with Renny Bennett so she was going to ruin my chances with you."

"Did you know it was her all along?"

"I got a message from Sam on Sunday that she'd gone missing. I wasn't a hundred percent sure it was her but I had a feeling."

"And you didn't tell me? You didn't think it was necessary to warn me that in the line of duty you'd pissed somebody off and now they were gunning for me?"

The way she'd said it told Trent he wasn't going to like the way this conversation was going.

"If there was something I could have warned you about, Tia, I would have. Believe me when I say I never wanted you hurt."

She sighed, then turned away from him. She couldn't think when he was so close and when he glared at her like that it was even harder. For the hours he'd been gone she'd paced and thought and thought and paced. The answers weren't clear because there were just too many questions. But from what she could squeeze out of Adam, this stalker of hers was connected to Trent and his job.

She wondered if being with Trent could possibly lead

to a repeat of the pain and suffering she'd gone through with Jake. Sure, death, at some point in time, knocked on everybody's door. But with Trent, working covert operations with terrorists in foreign countries or working cases with domestic criminals could cost him his life. In which case she'd be left alone. Again.

It was a terribly selfish thought, one she'd been fighting with for the last two hours, but still Tia couldn't shake it.

He touched her shoulders and she instinctively pulled away. "Is it always like this?" she asked from across the room.

"Like what?"

"The waiting and the worrying."

Trent sighed as if this on top of everything else was finally taking its toll. "It is what it is, Tia."

"And it's your job," she said turning to face him.

Slipping his hands into his pockets Trent eyed her closely. "My job is dangerous, yes. Could someone try to come after you again because of me?" He paused then nodded. "Yes. I'm not going to lie to you about the danger."

"I can at least thank you for that," she snapped, then dropped down into a chair near the window.

Trent moved to her, going down on his knee in front of her and taking her hands. "But what I can tell you is that I've never been as afraid as I was tonight. I've never feared anything when I'm working. Nothing," he emphasized the word by giving her a slight shake.

"And I was afraid…of losing you."

Tia froze all the questions and doubts that had been filtering through her mind. "But we're just lovers," she whispered.

"You don't believe that any more than I do," he told her.

"Adam said he admired me because I've always known what I want and I've always gone after it. Well, this time

I didn't know. I thought I wanted to sleep with you, once, maybe twice. I thought that would be enough."

Her heart had begun to beat faster, her mind reeling with his words.

"But it wasn't. I told you I didn't want love and marriage and a family of my own. But, I do, Tia. I want all that and then some. And I want it with you."

She was shaking her head. Part of her leaping for joy over his words and another part feeling the impending doom. "What are you saying, Trent?"

"I'm saying that I love you, baby. I've never loved another woman in my life but I know without a doubt that I love you. And while my job is very dangerous I know we can make this work."

She closed her eyes, sighed and opened them again. "I thought about this all day. How I would tell you this. I rehearsed the words over and over but now with everything that's happened I don't know where to begin."

"Just say what you feel," he directed.

She nodded, and took his advice. "I love you, too, Trent." He smiled and for a second she almost faltered. But there was one thing Tia was perfectly clear on was that love was not enough to spare the pain.

"But," she said and watched his smile falter. "It's not enough."

"What? Not enough?"

"Devlin called while you were out. He left a message that you were needed ASAP…in Dubai," she said matter-of-factly.

He was going to kick Devlin's ass! Never in all the time they'd worked together had he left a message with anyone about their assignments. Why now and why leave it with Tia?

"That has nothing to do with us," he started.

"Doesn't it? You've just been out tonight chasing down a stalker and Lord knows what else. Now, first thing tomorrow morning you're most likely going to board a plane heading into a foreign country where you have no idea what could be waiting for you. How do you expect me to deal with that?"

He didn't know. Ironically, though, he'd thought of this very scenario for years.

"We can make this work, Tia. I know we can."

She shook her head. "No. We can't. I won't." Standing, she moved away from him to avoid both his touch and his gaze. "I'm finally about to get myself together. Coming to terms with losing Jake and Jessica and with myself. It would be foolish of me to walk right into another situation that could cost me so much."

"You're not being fair. You can't predict the future any more than I can. Hell, you could get killed and then I'd be left alone. But that's no reason to live your life in a precautionary mode all the time. Come on, Tia. This is ridiculous!"

"What's ridiculous is that you can't see my side of this."

"And what side is that? Run scared and stay safe? No, I don't see the logic in that. I'm not a runner, I'm a fighter. And I thought you were, too."

"Then you don't know me well at all. I won't go through this all over again. And, no, I can't predict the future but I know that your job is dangerous, your life is dangerous. That will always be cause for me to worry. I can't live like that."

"Don't you mean you won't live like that?" He was walking toward her now. "You won't give us a chance because you're too afraid of being hurt. I'd say that was a typical female stance but I know how you hate to be stereotyped."

"You're an insensitive jerk," she said softly, wounded.

"No. I'm a fool for thinking that this one time I'd met

a woman who was different. But you're not, are you, Tia? You want everything from a man without sacrificing anything of yourself. Women always say it's the other way around but, you know, I don't believe it is. I'm pouring my heart out to you and you don't give a damn!"

"I didn't ask you to pour your heart out," she said and knew that sounded trite. Why couldn't he understand she was afraid? For him. For her. For what they could build only to lose.

"No. You only asked to be lovers. Well, we've done that so what now?"

They stood as if in a standoff, neither one of them sure of what to say next.

"Now you do what you do best. You do your job," she said solemnly, then turned, leaving him to stand alone in her room.

Chapter 16

Three weeks later

She was sick. She had the flu or a stomach virus or something.

Tia brushed her teeth, gargled with mouthwash, then padded back to her brand-new four-poster bed.

She'd stayed with Adam and Camille for two weeks before finding a terrific house just off the coast of Los Angeles. She'd left Vegas and all its terrible memories behind.

L.A. was only a few hours away so it didn't feel like that big of a move. But after all she'd been through, it was just the change she'd needed.

Camille wasn't terribly pleased but recognized Tia's need to get away. Jeanne had referred her to another therapist and she was keeping regular weekly appointments.

Except this week. Because of her sickness, she'd cancelled two appointments with the therapist and one early morning photo shoot for a Victoria's Secret lingerie ad. Her agent had reworked that one so that later this afternoon she was expected in the studio. And come hell or high water she was determined to be there.

Climbing into bed with her cup of now tepid tea, Tia pulled the covers up to her neck and burrowed deep under the covers. Her head hurt and she felt as if she were floating, no, falling down an endless flight of stairs. Her stomach still churned and she wondered if it might not be smarter to simply make her bed on the bathroom floor.

The last week had been a repeat of this, not really getting worse but definitely not getting better. Tomorrow would be day seven and if she was still feeling ill she'd resigned herself to finally calling the doctor.

Just when she'd begun to doze off her doorbell rang. Tia moaned, then decided if she kept quiet whoever was at the door would go away.

Bzzzzzzzz.

Wrong. Persistence was definitely not a virtue.

Climbing out of the bed, she found her robe and slippers and made her way out of the room and down the stairs to the front door.

Never would she have expected to see the smiling person on the other side.

"Noelle? What are you doing here?"

"And good morning, nice to see you, too," Noelle Vincent said, stepping into the house uninvited. "Long story short, Camille's worried and so is Ms. Beverly. I'm here scoping out new venues for Linc's expansion so I told them I'd stop by to make sure you're okay."

Noelle paused just as Tia closed the door. She was wearing big-framed dark sunglasses with a white jeweled rim that she pulled off slowly. Eyeing Tia up and down, she began to shake her head. "Oh, no, no, no."

"What?" Tia looked at herself. Her robe was satin, peach, a really good color for her. Her slippers, furry and white, her hair was pulled back courtesy of her latest bout in the bathroom retching up any and everything in her stomach. So what was Noelle staring at?

"You are tore up from the floor up."

Tia frowned. "I am not." Then self-conscious, she wrapped her arms around her waist. "And it's too early in the morning for anybody to look as pretty and pert as you do."

She walked away toward the living room, knowing that Noelle would follow her.

"No, dear, it is never too early to look good. You know that, you're the model."

"Models do not work 24/7."

"Looking at you I'd say they're on hiatus."

"Ha. Ha. Very funny," Tia quipped, then fell onto the couch, pulling her legs up behind her and lying down. "Welcome to my home, have a seat," she told Noelle, who stood looking down at her disapprovingly.

Noelle knelt and put her hand on Tia's forehead. "No fever," she said.

"Thank you, Florence Nightingale."

"Smart-ass mouth." Noelle continued to assess Tia. She sniffed. "Have you been throwing up?"

"What?" Tia sniffed. She'd washed her face, hands and brushed her teeth after her bathroom tryst.

"You look like hell but you smell like a bottle of mouthwash. Either you have a hangover or you've been puking."

Tia sighed, closing her eyes and trying to steady the

queasiness building in her stomach again. "Tell me again why you're here, Noelle. To be nosy, right?"

Noelle laughed. "Nope, not nosy, just considerate. Now, if you don't tell me what's wrong with you the phone call I make back to Camille will definitely ensure some level of nosiness on her part as she's going to hop on a plane and come see you for herself."

"Damn." Tia took another steadying breath. "I don't know what's wrong with me. Is that good enough for you? I've been sick for a couple of days. Vomiting, headaches, nausea."

Noelle had removed her jacket and was perched on the other end of the couch looking at Tia while she talked. Lifting slightly when she didn't hear a response, Tia glanced at Noelle. "What?"

Noelle smiled. "You don't have a clue, do you?"

"A clue about what?" Tia groaned and sat up, prepared to haul ass to the bathroom with the next painful wave in her stomach.

"You're pregnant, that's what."

Tia's head snapped in Noelle's direction. "I am not!" she said adamantly, then felt that wave and jumped up from the chair. There was a powder room on the lower level and Tia just made it in time to avoid an embarrassing mess.

She was leaning over the sink rinsing her mouth out when she heard Noelle's approach.

"You were saying?" she said with a knowing grin.

"I was saying that if I am pregnant you'll be the number one babysitter on my list."

The fear that Noelle might be absolutely right sank in and Tia felt like she'd finally hit the bottom of those stairs she'd been floating over these last few days. Hitting the floor with a resounding thud, she fainted.

* * *

"How are you, baby?" Beverly Donovan spoke into the phone while sitting on the deck looking at the early morning sunrise.

"I'm good, Mom. How are you and dad?" Trent asked, his voice a little scratchy.

Since when did her son start lying to her? "We're well."

"That's good. I just wanted to call and check up on you guys. How's Jade and the twins?"

"Torian and Tamala are beautiful. Linc is in heaven, you know."

"Yeah, I talked to him the day before yesterday."

And he talked to Adam almost every day. Never, and she believed the word, never had Trent called home this many times while being on an assignment. Something was definitely wrong and she knew what it was.

"Are things going all right with work?"

"He's a slippery one but then we knew that since we've been tracking him for five years. But we're closing in."

"So you'll be home soon?"

He was quiet.

"Trent?"

"I'm not sure I'm coming home, to Vegas I mean."

"What? Why?"

"I've been thinking about opening that P.I. firm with Sam Desdune. If so, I'll probably head back east for a while to see how he's running the operation there, then settle on a location on the west coast."

"Oh," she said waiting patiently for him to get to the real reason he'd called. "That sounds like a smart plan if it's what you really want."

He sighed. "Yeah. I think it's time to get out of this game. The traveling and instability, I'm getting a little old for it."

Beverly nodded. "So you're ready to settle down…in one place I mean?"

"I think it's time."

He sounded lonely, and her mother's instinct wished it could reach through that phone and hug him. But Trent was her most independent child. He made his own decisions in his own time or he didn't do it. That's why she kept silent and only hugged him three weeks ago when he'd come to the house to say he was leaving. She'd seen something in his eyes that day she'd never seen before and knew it could only be one thing.

Her baby had finally fallen in love.

Of course she'd talked to Camille who'd informed her that Tia and Trent were no longer seeing each other. Tia hadn't given Camille all the details except to say that it just wasn't going to work. She didn't want to be sitting on pins and needles wondering if he'd come back to her dead or alive.

To a certain extent Beverly could understand the young woman's fears. She certainly worried each and every day that Trent was away. But she'd learned to have faith that whatever was meant to be would be. As she'd told Tia before, God did not make mistakes.

"It might be time you stopped calling everybody but the one you really want to talk to," Beverly said quietly.

"She doesn't want to talk to me. She made that perfectly clear."

"And what do you want?"

Trent was so quiet for so long she thought they'd been disconnected.

"Trent?"

"I want her."

She sighed. "You've never backed down from something you wanted before. Why now?"

"Because I love her enough to want her to be happy. And if she's happier without me," he cleared his throat. "If she's happier without me then that's the way it will be."

"I don't think either one of you is happy and it's high time somebody did something about it."

"Don't worry about it, Mom. I've accepted the way things have to be."

But Beverly hadn't. Those two belonged together and the minute Trent stepped back on American soil she was going to make sure they knew it.

Camille had warned Adam not to call. What she'd told him this afternoon was in the deepest of confidence. He couldn't betray her.

He shouldn't betray her.

But Trent was his brother and he deserved to know.

"Donovan?"

Adam moved into his home office after closing and locking the door. Camille was somewhere in the house so he'd used his cell phone. Locking the door ensured she didn't walk in on his conversation.

"Hey, man, what's up?"

"Adam? What's going on? Are Mom and Dad okay?" Trent asked, concern lacing his voice.

"They're fine," he answered quickly. This was the first time Adam had ever called Trent while he was on assignment. But circumstances called for drastic measures.

"Then why are you calling?"

"Is this a bad time?"

"I'm in the Middle East hunting a terrorist. What do you mean is this a bad time? What's going on?"

Adam took a deep breath and said it before he changed his mind for the billionth time. "Tia's pregnant."

There was a lot of background noise and Adam called out to Trent wondering if the line had been broken.

"Say that again," he finally spoke.

"Noelle went out to L.A. for work and she stopped by to check on her. Tia was really sick. For the next two days Noelle stayed with her and finally convinced her to go to the doctor. She found out she was pregnant yesterday."

"Did she tell you to call me?"

Adam didn't answer.

"Adam, did she tell you to call me?"

"It doesn't matter. You two are being ridiculous. She's carrying your child, man. You need to get your ass back here and take care of her. Make things right with her."

Thousands of miles away Trent pinched the bridge of his nose. They'd captured Clobol last night but not without bloodshed. Josh was hurt, his truck barely escaping the explosives that booby-trapped Clobol's hideaway. Baywatch had been shot twice while they attempted to apprehend the suspected terrorist. It had been a rough night and now this.

"I'm not what she wants," he said finally, feeling the all too familiar sting of rejection.

The day Tia had told him they had no future had been worse than all the deaths he'd witnessed, all the lives he'd taken. The pain had been unbearable, intolerable, until he'd had no choice but to walk away from her. Because to stay would have been dangerous for them both.

"That's bull and you know it! You've both got some pretty stupid hang-ups if you ask me. And this baby is just the sign you two need to get off your stupid stools and act like mature adults who love each other."

Was this his baby brother talking? Was this the same one

who'd wiped snot on his shirt sleeve until he was in middle school? When had Adam grown into such a man?

"Adam, I appreciate what you're trying to do, but—"

"Don't give me that. You know what the right thing to do is, Trent. I don't have to tell you. She's carrying your child and I thought you should know."

Trent was silent, letting this entire conversation digest. "Camille's going to kick your ass for telling me this, you know that right?"

Adam chuckled. "That's why I'm counting on you to make things right so I'll have some leverage when she finds out."

There really wasn't a choice, Trent conceded. If Tia was pregnant with his child he had to go to her. The fact that they couldn't make it together was their decision and he would live with it. But his child...his *child*... Trent never thought about having kids of his own, never realized he'd wanted them. But with this new knowledge he felt a warmth in his chest, a tingling of pride that he and a woman like Tia had created a child, a baby that would call him "Daddy."

"I'll be home as soon as I can," he said, then disconnected the line and hurried to pack.

Chapter 17

Sleep didn't come easy to Tia these days. It had been almost a week since she'd found out she was pregnant. Yes, pregnant with Trent Donovan's baby.

How bad could one person's luck actually be?

Tia felt as if she had a permanent hex placed on her personal life. Her career was in full swing but she'd made an error in judgment the night she'd invited Trent to her bed. Initially she'd thought she could handle it, she'd done so before.

But those other men weren't Trent. Only Trent could get her so worked up she'd forget to remind him about protection. He'd apologized afterward, she remembered, and looked genuinely remorseful. But the fact was, they'd gotten carried away. Both of them. So it was a mutual mess up.

Resting a hand to her still-flat stomach she sighed. A mutual mess up that would now forever be a reminder of the short time they'd had together.

Tia was hardly kidding herself. She and Trent were over. She'd told him that she could not stay in a relationship with him, he'd accepted and left. But then what had she thought he would do? Did she want him to quit his job to be with her? Would that have made her happy? Probably not, she decided. That man loves his job.

She stared at the phone wondering if today would be the day she tried to contact him. Shaking her head she looked away. No, not today. She needed more time to acclimate herself to this new development before pulling Trent into the equation.

It was bad enough Noelle and Camille knew. If and when the rest of the Donovan clan found out they would circle her like a pack. Because that's what they were: a family, a strong, close-knit family who did what they had to do for each other.

Tia had no doubt that would include telling Trent about her situation.

No, she was definitely not ready for that.

"Tia?" Noelle called as she knocked lightly on her bedroom door.

Noelle had been with her for the past week. She'd stayed in L.A. under the pretense of casino business, but Tia knew that it was at Camille's urging that Noelle stayed and kept an eye on her. Which for the most part didn't bother Tia. She hadn't realized how difficult it would be to go back to her solitary life after having the Donovans under foot for the past month. Tia had to admit she really enjoyed them.

"Come in," Tia answered, turning from the window she'd been staring out of.

"Hey, how you feeling?" Noelle asked, first peeking her head inside, then coming fully into the room.

Tia really liked Noelle. She was fun to be around and

compassionate and she was gorgeous, there was no doubt about that. She'd assumed Noelle had a boyfriend but from the sounds of her stilted conversations with some man named Luther, it wasn't a match made in heaven. Still, she was sure once Noelle officially dropped him she'd have many other men at her door.

"I'm better. Still a little tired though."

"Well, the doctor said you had a virus on top of your pregnancy. So you're probably going to need a while to get over that."

"Yeah, you're right. What are you up to today?" she asked when Noelle hadn't taken her usual seat on the foot of Tia's bed while they talked. "Is it time for you to get back to the casino?"

Noelle looked at her strangely. "Why? Are you putting me out?"

"Of course not," Tia smiled. "You just look so serious today. I was wondering if you were hating to leave L.A."

"No. That's not it."

"Then what's going on? You can talk to me, Noelle. For all the help you've given me these past few days, you can tell me anything."

Noelle sighed heavily, then looked back to Tia. "I have to tell you something that I know you're not going to like. And I'm only going to tell you because I think you should know what's about to happen. We've become pretty good friends and as a friend—"

She interrupted. "Just tell me, Noelle."

"I know you weren't expecting this and that's why I wanted to say something to you first."

"Noelle, what are you trying to say?"

"She's trying to tell you that I'm back."

Tia froze. His voice was like thick honey slipping all

over her body. Only she couldn't afford to let herself get swallowed in that funnel again. Turning slowly, she let her eyes sweep the room until they found him. He looked even better than ever. He wore jeans and a T-shirt that fit him too well to be legal and an expression that said he had a lot on his mind. Tia swallowed hard.

"Are you going to be all right?" Noelle had come to stand beside her, dropping a hand to her shoulder. It was good to have a friend, another one, she thought. Camille—bless her heart—had probably told her fiancé about Tia's pregnancy because she loved him so very much and wanted no secrets between them. And because the Donovans were thicker than thieves, Adam had most likely told Trent. She couldn't be angry with any of them. But she was nervous as hell.

Facing Trent with this news was inevitable, however, she would have liked to be a little more prepared. Instead, here she was sitting near the window in her bedroom looking as if she'd been through a world war.

"It's fine, Noelle. Don't worry about it."

Tia stood because the last thing she wanted was to appear weak in front of Trent. He expected more than that.

"I'm not going to hurt her, Noelle," he said with a look of impatience.

Noelle sauntered toward the door. "Who said I was worried about *you* hurting *her*," she quipped on her way out.

The corner of his mouth lifted as he shook his head and closed the door behind her. Tia watched his movements, noting the flex of muscles in his arms and his back as he turned. Her gaze continued to roam over him until she realized she was checking to see if he'd been hurt while he was away.

It had been four weeks since she'd last seen him and not one day had gone by that she hadn't thought of him, of his safety. In fact, her nights had been filled with sleepless hours as she'd imagined any and everything possible happening to him. Wasn't this the very thing she'd hoped to avoid by breaking up with him?

"How are you?" he asked, leaning against the door.

He'd folded his arms over his chest as she'd perused him. He was so damned arrogant, she thought. And so damned fine.

"I'm good. How are you?"

His heart hammered in his chest with the force of a battering ram and he thought he was going to be sick. He'd say he wasn't doing too well.

Trent had flown directly to L.A. not wanting to waste a moment by stopping in Vegas first. He'd needed to see her, to set his eyes on her once again. She was as beautiful today as she was that night in Adam's house. She'd been crying then, today she looked as if the crying had stopped but the hurting hadn't. He wanted to reach out and touch her, to hold her in his arms but knew that would be too much, too soon.

"I'm fine."

"That's good."

"I like the house," he said looking around the room. "What made you buy something on the coast?"

She gazed briefly out the window to the breathtaking view of cliffs and water. He'd admired the area as he'd driven here from the airport, still unable to believe she'd actually purchased a house instead of moving into another apartment. And she'd bought furniture, lots of furniture. Downstairs looked as if she'd lived here more than two years. It was comfortable, plush and peaceful. Home.

Turning back to him, she shrugged. "I've always liked the water."

"So do I," he said and watched her look of surprise. For

as much as he loved this woman he realized how little they really knew about each other. Trent knew there would never be another woman to claim his heart the way she had. And his intention had been to come here and fight for her. Now, seeing her, in this place she'd built for herself, this slice of happiness she'd managed to carve out despite the roller-coaster ride of a relationship he'd given her, he didn't know if he could.

"Let's not beat around the bush," she said finally. "I really don't have the strength for it."

He took a tentative step toward her. "How do you feel? I heard you've been sick."

She tilted her head, her braids that had been pulled back from her face shifted. His fingers itched to touched them, to take her into his arms.

"Did you hear that or did you call the doctor and ask for my records?"

He wasn't sure how much of that question was to be taken lightly, so he shrugged. "Honestly, a little of both."

She nodded, the edges of her lips turning upward.

"Adam didn't give me a whole lot of information and I needed to know."

"You needed to know what I was keeping from you again. That's a real bad habit you have, Trent. People are entitled to their secrets if that's what they want."

"I needed to know that you were okay, Tia. That's all." Trent stopped, took a deep breath and tried to start over. He really did not want to fight with her. "Were you planning to keep my baby a secret? If so, you probably shouldn't have told Camille."

"Camille is loyal if nothing else." She shook her head and moved to the window. "No. I wasn't planning to keep the baby a secret. I would have liked to tell you in my own time but I guess this is as good as any. We can get it over with."

"Is that what we're doing now? Getting it over with?"

"I don't know what you want me to say, Trent. I've never known what you wanted me to say."

"You could say that you're happy to be carrying my child and that maybe we can make this work." He held his breath the moment the words came out.

She turned back to him. "I am happy to be carrying your child," she said with a wistful smile. "Two months ago the thought of carrying another baby was as fearful to me as being involved in another car accident. I'd vowed that I would never get pregnant again. And then you came along with your arrogant smile and deadly hands and wham! I'm pregnant."

He chuckled because she'd made what they had sound so normal, so happenstance.

"I didn't think about having a baby, either. But I've got to tell you I'm pretty pumped about it now." To hell with all these pretenses. He moved to her, touching a hand to the small of her back. "I'm more than pumped, I'm ecstatic. You're having my baby. The woman I finally fell in love with is carrying my child and she's more beautiful than ever. I couldn't be happier."

Lifting a hand to cup his cheek she smiled. At that moment Trent knew instinctively what she was about to say wasn't going to be good.

"You're going to be a good father, I know. And I'm going to do my best to be a good mother. This will be one lucky child."

"We'll be great together." He heard himself saying the words even as she shook her head.

"No. What I said before you left still stands, Trent. Us as a couple is just not going to work."

He stiffened. "You mean you don't want it to work."

"I don't want to experience it falling apart."

"You don't know that it will. Look, Tia, I know that my job is dangerous but it would be so even if I were a fire-fighter, a police officer. Hell, cab drivers even have it rough. It's called living in the real world. Things happen that we have no control over."

"But I do have control over this, don't you see? I realize that now. I can choose to take a different route. I'm carrying your child, which means a part of you will always be con-nected to me. I'll have to be content with that. You can't expect me to endure the waiting, the not knowing."

Her eyes filled with tears and Trent struggled with wanting to pull her close and wanting to shake some sense into her. He'd thought she'd battled this and was on her way to winning. This fear that had such a fierce hold on every-thing she did. He'd thought the therapy and the house had all been working toward that end. How could she be standing here telling him that she wouldn't be with him because she was afraid he would die?

"I can't do it, Trent. I just can't. I know it sounds crazy and I know you don't understand. But it's too much, it's too soon."

"It's been two years, Tia."

"It's been twenty-six months, a week and a day. It's still in here." She patted a hand over her heart. "I carry it with me just as I'm carrying your child. Just as I carried the thought of you getting shot or blown up every second you were away."

"Baby, I'm fine. I'm here right now with you. I'm trying—"

She moved away from him. "You're trying to make me do what you want. But sometimes, Trent, we don't al-ways get what we want. Sometimes we just have to deal with what we have. And all I have right now is a bunch of memories that are partly good but mostly tragic. And I don't know how to deal with them or if I'll ever move past them. No, I don't blame myself anymore and I don't plan on living my life in a shell any longer. But these are just small steps, ones that I have to take to get me to a better place."

"And I can't be a part of that? Is that what you're saying? I'm hindering your healing?" He couldn't believe her words, didn't want to hear them. But they were there, thrown out and sticking between them like a beaten stump.

The tears had escaped, making tracks down her pretty face, swiping at his heart with vicious strokes.

"I'm saying that it's too much. I can't do all this right now. I need time and space and I don't really expect you to wait around."

She hadn't asked him to wait around. He would have, for her he'd wait an eternity. Hell, he felt like he already had. But Trent was nothing if he wasn't logical. She'd made some good points. She needed to heal, completely.

In two months he had put her in the same position she'd been in before, pregnant and with a man considering a committed relationship. Feeling the fear of a repeat performance wasn't that far-fetched. He doubted he would feel that way but then he was the one who had avoided relationships because he was afraid of leaving his family. In a sense, he and Tia were birds of the same feather. So he couldn't really begrudge her honesty. No matter how much it hurt.

"No. You can't expect me to wait around," he said tightly. "But you can expect me to be a part of my child's life. You can't take that from me."

She shook her head as the tears continued to flow. "No. I would never do that."

He inhaled, then let out a deep breath. "Well, then. I guess I should go."

When she didn't speak again he moved to the door. Pulling it open he stopped. If this were to be the last time he could speak to her this freely, the last time he could express himself to her before they officially moved into their baby mama and baby daddy status then he wouldn't let it go to waste. He couldn't.

"I wanted to marry you, Tia. I wanted to give you some of the happiness that you lost. We could have been great together. A great family."

And then he was gone. Tia threw herself onto the bed and sobbed as she hadn't done in twenty-six months, a week and a day.

Chapter 18

"One day at a time, Tia. That's all we can do is take one day at a time," Madeline St. Claire spoke through the phone. Her baby was hurting, again. Only this time the pain had been self-induced.

She hadn't met this Trent Donovan, but she'd heard Tia speaking of him for weeks. In fact, she'd planned a trip to L.A. to see her daughter and to possibly meet this man who had captured her heart.

When she called Tia to tell her this she was surprised to hear the complete desolation in her voice. Now, an hour later they were still on the phone. She, trying to console and talk some sense into her only child and Tia trying to protect herself from fate. One of them was fighting a futile battle.

"He's a soldier, Mom. Any one of his assignments could end badly."

"Jake wasn't a soldier, baby. He was just a man and man

only has a certain amount of time on earth. It's the way God planned it."

"Well, I want to make some plans of my own. Can't I do that?"

"Yes, you can. But you need to accept that you have no control over whether or not those plans actually come to fruition. It's about living the life you've been given in the time it's given to you, Tia. If you love this man, and I can hear it in your voice that you do, then you should be with him. Nothing should stop you from grabbing hold of that love with both hands. Nothing."

"But what if love isn't enough?" Tia argued.

"It all starts with love. You're carrying his child, Tia. A part of him is living and breathing in you. Don't you think that happened for a reason?"

"The same reason that I carried Jessica and she died."

"That was God's will, and no matter what you or I say or do, God's will will be done. Staying away from Trent won't change that. When it's his time he'll be taken. When it's yours you'll go, too—albeit kicking and screaming with your stubborn self," Madeline said with a light chuckle.

Tia couldn't help but smile herself. If ever she wanted brutal honesty, it would come from her mother.

"I'm scared, Mom."

"I know it and I'm sorry for it. Remember that Christmas when your father bought you that pretty pink bicycle without the training wheels? You told him you couldn't possibly ride a bike without the extras on it." Madeline sighed at the memory.

"You're little face was so worried I thought you'd never model again because the crinkles would be permanently embedded in your forehead. And when I touched your shoulders you jumped. I hugged you to me and your little heart just about pounded out of your chest. You remember what I whispered in your ear?"

One tear ran down Tia's cheek even as she smiled, the memory clear in her mind. "You said if I didn't get on that bike and ride like the wind I'd be stuck in that house in Arizona for the rest of my life while other kids grew up and moved on. Then you said that you and Daddy had plans for my room once I graduated so I needed to get my butt on that bike and stop being a baby."

Both women were laughing now.

"Now I'm not there to hug you tight, but if I were, you know I would do just that. And then I'd tell you to get off your butt and go get that man. Your daddy and I have plans for more than one grandbaby from you."

Tia had hung up the phone thanking her mother for all her advice but still feeling like she'd made the right decision, no matter how painful it was.

She took a shower and changed her clothes. She was hungry so she'd left her room and went downstairs to find something to eat. She hadn't expected company, hadn't even known she had company. But there they were, two thirds of the Triple Threat Donovans.

"Hi, Tia," Adam spoke first coming to give her a hug.

She took the hug letting the feel of support wash over her. "Hi, Adam."

He released her and she looked to Linc. "You left Jade and the babies?"

After hugging her he chuckled. "Mom's staying with them. I had to come out to check on my star employee and the locations she'd spotted for the Gramercy expansion."

"Oh," she said.

"Here, sit down. Can I get you something?" Linc offered.

"No. It's okay. I was just going to make a sandwich."

"I'll get it," Adam said.

"Camille let you out of her sight?"

Adam smiled over his shoulder as he reached across the counter to get the bread. "If she could have come herself she would have, but she's having some factory issues that can't be ignored. Deli?"

"Ah, no. Peanut butter and jelly."

"My kind of girl," Linc smiled.

Tia ate her sandwich, while Linc ate one, as well, and Adam munched on potato chips. It was a homely scene and yet an uncomfortable one. She knew they weren't here strictly for social reasons, so she figured the quicker she got to the bottom of it, the better.

"So did you come with Trent?"

"Are you kidding?" Adam finished chewing. "He would have killed us."

"We took the flight in after him," Linc smiled.

She nodded. "Why?"

"Because you two have the hardest heads this side of the U.S.," Adam said in his sincere but brutally honest tone.

"I don't know what you're talking about," Tia said with slight annoyance. "Trent and I have made a mature decision."

"You're skirting around each other and your feelings as if it were a land mine. You're both crazy."

Linc interrupted. "Crazy in love."

Tia sighed, letting her elbows rest on the table. "Love is not enough."

"It is when you make it enough," Linc said, taking one of her hands in his. "He quit his job, Tia."

Her head shot up. "What?"

"He's leaving the special ops team to open the P.I. firm with Sam Desdune."

"But he loves his job," she said quietly.

"He loves you more," Linc said simply.

"No. He was considering going into business with Sam long before me. He didn't do this for me." Because if he had she didn't know how she felt about that. How she would live with that.

"True, he'd been struggling with the decision. But right before he found out you were pregnant, his decision was made. He came back here to tell you that, hoping it would win you back."

"He didn't tell me. Damn him, he didn't say a word!"

Adam laughed. "That's Trent for you. He wanted you to know the job change was about you and him. It was about the life he wants to lead. The baby is icing on the cake."

Tia stood and paced the room. He hadn't told her about the job. And he could have, when she told him that was the reason she wouldn't be with him, he could have told her hoping that would have made a difference. Would it?

He'd said that no matter what his occupation the world was a dangerous place. That was certainly true, looking at all the innocent people being shot or killed by senseless violence.

"He didn't tell me that he'd planned to become a P.I. That we could have some semblance of a normal life. Why? Why didn't he tell me?"

"Because despite his pushy, arrogant ways, Trent isn't about making people do anything they don't want to do. That's not how he operates. If he felt that you truly didn't want to be with him he wasn't going to resort to compromise to get you to stay. He's stubborn that way. Go figure."

"He's honorable that way," Linc added. "And if you love him half as much as we know he loves you, you'll understand exactly why he didn't tell you."

Leaning against the counter, Tia combated the thumping of her heart. She loved Trent every bit as much as they believed he loved her. If not more. He hadn't told her because he wanted her to heal. That's what she'd said she needed to do and despite how he felt, how much he'd changed for her, he'd agreed.

The incessant tears were back again but this time not for pain. She was happy to have found a man who loved and cared for her well-being so much. Happy to be carrying his baby and…

"Where is he?" she asked suddenly.

Linc lifted his arm and looked at his watch. "I'd say he's on his way to the airport. His flight back to Vegas leaves in about twenty minutes."

"Twenty minutes," she whispered, wiping quickly at her tears. "Okay. I can do this. I can do this."

Adam was already standing, reaching into his pocket for the keys. "We can do this," he said grabbing hold of her elbow and moving toward the door. "I'm driving."

While in her room enjoying her pity party Tia had no idea the beautifully sunny day had turned into a heavy spring shower. She watched as raindrops attacked the windshield and traffic slowed to an annoying crawl.

Her heart pounded in rhythm with her hand on her leg. She had to make it in time. She just had to. She'd been foolish and blind and, yes, foolish. Admitting she was wrong was going to be hard but hopefully it would be worth it.

When they finally arrived at the airport Tia looked frantically for a domestic flight going back to Vegas when Linc pulled her in another direction.

"He's a Donovan, remember—flying usually entails using the company jet," Linc reminded her.

She had forgotten. Trent seemed so normal you'd never guess he was a multimillionaire. Except when you were being rushed through the swinging door of the private hangar space.

Linc and Adam checked at the counter, then came back to her. "He's boarding. You can wait until the jet returns and go to Vegas."

"Or you can call him," Adam offered.

"No!" she said adamantly. "It has to be now." She looked toward the door and made a dash for it.

The minute she was outside the rain pelted her skin with a steady beat. Her shirt immediately stuck to her chest, her jean capris growing heavier as she moved. She wore tennis shoes and no jacket but none of that mattered.

In the distance she could see the plane and that the hatch was still open. Continuing to run toward it, she searched the area for any sign of Trent. He was probably already on the plane. Well, then she would get on the plane, too. Nothing was going to stop her from saying what she had to say to him.

She was running, her only focus, her destination the plane, when she was grabbed around the waist by a strong arm.

"Are you crazy? What are you doing out here?" Trent asked when he turned her to face him.

Tia looked up, her vision blurred by the raindrops in her eyes. "I was coming for you," she said breathlessly. "I had to see you before you left."

"Tia, it's a freakin' monsoon out here. Get back inside before you get sick again," he yelled over the loudness of the plane's engine.

"No!" she yelled back, jerking out of his grasp. "I have something to say and you're going to listen."

His face said he didn't like it but the way he folded his arms said he wasn't going to fight her anymore.

"You should have told me about the P.I. firm, Trent.

When you came into my room you should have told me about your plans."

"Would that have made a difference?"

She hesitated only a second. "Yes."

"Then that's why I didn't tell you."

"But you said you wanted us to be together?"

"I want us to be together if that's what you want, not because I'm quitting the military and you feel that's safer for me. I don't want you on a bargain."

Just like she'd thought. Just like his brothers had said. He was too damned honorable.

She rolled her eyes skyward praying that what she was about to do was the right thing. "I want to be with you," she said wiping water from her eyes. At this point she couldn't tell if they were tears or not.

"Why?" he asked stoically.

"Because I love you."

"And you're not afraid that something might happen to me?"

"I'd be lying if I said I wasn't."

He sighed, then turned his head away from her.

Tia took a step closer to him, reached up and touched his chin until he looked at her. "But I'm dying without you," she said simply.

"These last few weeks have been the hardest of my life. I realize now it's because you weren't with me. Not just logistically, but here," she tapped her heart. "You weren't here because I wouldn't allow you to be. I wanted so much to protect myself, to keep from feeling the hurt of loneliness again. But all I did was throw my new happiness away."

"Tia," he began and she put her fingers over his lips to quiet him.

"No. Let me finish." He touched a hand to her wrist and she continued.

"You were right when you told me I needed to get some help. And you were right when you said that living and losing was just life. I guess I've known that all along. I was just so afraid. I've never been led by fear before but it felt safer for me. Until now. Until you.

"I love you more than I fear losing you. I need you more than I need to feel safe. You are my heart, my every-thing and I don't care what job you do, that fact won't change. I'd worry about you overseas or here, whether we were together or not."

Now there were tears, she knew because her vision had grown even blurrier although the rain had slackened to a steady drizzle. She was soaked and so was Trent and yet they stood on the tarmac as if they were the only two people in the world.

"Trent Donovan, will you marry me?"

"You are one stubborn, defiant woman, Tia St. Claire."

"Is that a *yes* or a *no?*"

Trent smiled. As if she'd even had to ask for clarification. When he'd seen her running through that door he'd stopped talking to the pilot. She was beautiful, her hair flowing behind her, her clothes sticking to her curvy body and she was coming to him, for him.

In all his life Trent had known women who were either attracted to his good looks or his hefty bank account. And he'd accepted that to the degree that it got him into their beds.

But on this rainy day, in this airport, he'd seen a woman coming for him, for Trent Donovan the man, and he'd been overwhelmed.

"You are gorgeous, on the inside and out." He wrapped

his arms around her waist, pulling her against his body. "You are strong and intelligent and the best kisser I've ever met."

She chuckled, just as he'd wanted her to.

"And I love you more than going off to fight a war. I need you more than I need to pick up a gun and catch the bad guy."

He leaned forward and touched his lips lightly to hers. "Yes, I'll marry you, baby," he whispered and kissed her again, this time stroking his tongue over her lower lip.

"I'll marry you and I'll love you and I'll heal you. We'll heal each other. You are my sunshine and my rain, my world."

A love that's out of this world…

Cosmic Rendezvous

Favorite author

Robyn Amos

For aerospace engineer Shelly London, a top-secret space project could be her big break—until she butts heads with sexy hotshot astronaut Lincoln Ripley, who launches her hormones right into orbit. Lincoln's got a double mission: catch a saboteur…then take off with Shelly for a rendezvous with love.

"Lilah's List is…a fun story that holds one's interest from page one."
—*Romantic Times BOOKreviews*

Coming the first week of April 2009 wherever books are sold.

KIMANI™
ROMANCE

www.kimanipress.com
www.myspace.com/kimanipress   KPRA1080409

He's an irresistible recipe—for trouble!

Sugar RUSH

elaine overton

Life is sweet for bakery owner Sophie Mayfield.
She's saved her family business from a takeover, and
hired talented baker Eliot Wright to help sales. Eliot
is as appealing—and oh-so-chocolate-fine—as he is
hardworking. But when Sophie discovers Eliot is not
what he seems, Eliot must regain Sophie's trust—and
prove he's her permanent sweet spot.

*Coming the first week of April 2009
wherever books are sold.*

KIMANI™
ROMANCE

www.kimanipress.com
www.myspace.com/kimanipress

KPEO1110409

REQUEST YOUR FREE BOOKS!

2 FREE NOVELS
PLUS 2 FREE GIFTS!

KIMANI™
ROMANCE

Love's ultimate destination!

YES! Please send me 2 FREE Kimani™ Romance novels and my 2 FREE gifts (gifts are worth about $10). After receiving them, if I don't wish to receive any more books, I can return the shipping statement marked "cancel." If I don't cancel, I will receive 4 brand-new novels every month and be billed just $4.69 per book in the U.S. or $5.24 per book in Canada, plus 25¢ shipping and handling per book and applicable taxes, if any*. That's a savings of over 20% off the cover price! I understand that accepting the 2 free books and gifts places me under no obligation to buy anything. I can always return a shipment and cancel at any time. Even if I never buy another book from Kimani Press, the two free books and gifts are mine to keep forever.

168 XDN EF2D   368 XDN EF3T

Name	(PLEASE PRINT)

Address	Apt. #

City	State/Prov.	Zip/Postal Code

Signature (if under 18, a parent or guardian must sign)

Mail to **The Reader Service:**
IN U.S.A.: P.O. Box 1867, Buffalo, NY 14240-1867
IN CANADA: P.O. Box 609, Fort Erie, Ontario L2A 5X3

Not valid to current subscribers of Kimani Romance books.

Want to try two free books from another line?
Call 1-800-873-8635 or visit www.morefreebooks.com.

* Terms and prices subject to change without notice. N.Y. residents add applicable sales tax. Canadian residents will be charged applicable provincial taxes and GST. Offer not valid in Quebec. This offer is limited to one order per household. All orders subject to approval. Credit or debit balances in a customer's account(s) may be offset by any other outstanding balance owed by or to the customer. Please allow 4 to 6 weeks for delivery. Offer available while quantities last.

Your Privacy: Kimani Press is committed to protecting your privacy. Our Privacy Policy is available online at www.eHarlequin.com or upon request from the Reader Service. From time to time we make our lists of customers available to reputable third parties who may have a product or service of interest to you. If you would prefer we not share your name and address, please check here. ☐

KROM08R

A dazzling story of a woman forced to decide where her heart really lies...

AWARD-WINNING AUTHOR

ADRIANNE BYRD

Love
takes time

All her life, Alyssa Jansen has loved handsome, wealthy Quentin Dwayne Hinton—a man who barely knows she exists. Now after years away in France, Alyssa's back, and Q is seeing her in a whole new light. But so is his brother Sterling, a handsome and passionate man who is willing to give Alyssa what she wants. Suddenly Alyssa must choose between a fairy tale come true and a new, unexpected love....

Coming the first week of April 2009 wherever books are sold.

"The Madaris family is one that fans will
never tire of!"
—*Romantic Times BOOKreviews*

NEW YORK TIMES BESTSELLING AUTHOR

BRENDA JACKSON

SURRENDER

A Madaris Family Novel

Military brat Nettie Brooms has vowed never
to become involved with a military man. But
Ashland Sinclair, a marine colonel, has very
different ideas about the sexy restaurant owner.
Now Nettie's wondering how a man she swore
she would avoid could so easily test her resolve
by igniting a passion she can't walk away from.

Available the first week of April 2009 wherever books are sold.

ARABESQUE®

www.kimanipress.com
www.myspace.com/kimanipress

KPBJI360409